Bob Moats

I0567280

Reunion Murders

1

Reunion Murders

This book is licensed for your personal use only. This book may not be re-sold or given away to other people. If you would like to share this book with another person, please purchase an additional copy for each recipient. If you're reading this book and did not purchase it, or it was not purchased for your use only, please purchase your own copy. Thank you for respecting the hard work of this author.

ISBN – 978-0-9960845-4-3

For information and address:
Magic 1 Productions
P.O. Box 524, Fraser MI 48026-0524
Website: http://murdernovels.com
Cover by Bob Moats

Bob Moats

Other Jim Richards series books by Bob Moats

(In Series Order)
Classmate Murders
Vegas Showgirl Murders
Dominatrix Murders
Mistress Murders
Bridezilla Murders
Magic Murders
Strip Club Murders
Made-for-TV Murders
Mystery Cruise Murders
Talk Show Murders
Sin City Murders
Black Widow Murders
Vegas Vigilante Murders
Area 51 Murders
Mortuary Murders
Hypnotic Murders
Sunshine State Murders
Blue Suede Murders
Honky Tonk Murders
Dark Carnival Murders
Lipstick Murders
Pasta Murders
Talent Show Murders
Shyster Murders
Campground Murders
Network Murders
Reunion Murders
Big Apple Murders
Kennel Murders
Trick or Treat Murders
Santa Murders

For a preview or to purchase a book, go to
http://murdernovels.com

3

What a few people are saying about Murder Novels by Bob Moats

Mr. Moats, I just got your novel "Classmate Murders" and have to let you know, I read it in one evening. That is the first book I have ever done that with. That was the most enjoyable book I have ever read. I just started reading e-books, and reading again, after getting my wife a Kindle. This book was my 12th, and the best. I just got Las Vegas Showgirls to (read) tomorrow evening. I look forward to reading many of your books in this series. I have been searching for an author and books that were fun, entertaining reads. Your books are just the ticket.

Regards, A new fan, Bill from South Carolina

****

Another very nice comment submitted through my website from Micki P.:

"I recently was given a kindle for my 60th birthday. The first book I downloaded was the Classmate Murders and have now read every one of the them. Today I started on the Fatal Rejection series. Thank you for the wonderful ride with Jim and Penny and all the rest of the troop. I have laughed and giggled thru the stories, my poor family gave me the strangest looks! Now I really want a little Yorkie!! Fatal Rejection so far is another great read! I will be looking out for more of Jim Richards and since you are my #1 Author, anything of yours I can find."

Extra special thanks to:

Special thanks to Val Brooks who edited this book and for her great suggestions.

Thanks to the beta readers Cindy Gross Valstad, Susan Houghton and Al Norris.

Thank you to all the people who purchased this book. I hope you enjoy it as much as I enjoyed writing it for my faithful readers.

The Jim Richards Family of Readers is listed in the back of the book.

Cover by Bob Moats, photo by Rita Meinburg.

My thanks to Shirley Davies, Ken Boggs, Sandy Sillman, Roland Hansen and Karen Meinburg Richwine for allowing me to use their images on the cover and I included them in the book as characters. There are a number of other people mentioned in the book who are all friends from Facebook. My thanks to them also.

Reunion Murders by Bob Moats

Chapter 1

The man hobbled down the stairs, slowly taking one step at a time. His leg was aching from his childhood injuries that now developed into arthritis. He hated getting old. He ambled to the door on the side of the basement, and with a key from his wallet he unlocked the door. He went in and over to the desk that sat along one wall, turning on the desk light. He picked up his prescription bottle and popped out a couple pills that the doctors told him would ease the pain. He opened the bottle of whiskey from a shelf and downed a shot glass of the liquid to wash down the pills.

He turned to the wall opposite the desk and went to it. He turned on another light, brightening a corkboard filled with photos. He stood, examining one particular photo of people grouped in the center. One woman and two men were of his interest.

He got closer to study them. Then, he pulled out a thin knife and started to stab the people in the photo, one at a time. One after another, right through their bodies, close to the heart.

"Soon, I will make you regret what you did to me," he said to the photo.

~~*~~

The invitation was addressed to the home of Jim Richards and his wife Penny Wickens.

Penny was not home when the mail came. She was interviewing guests on her TV talk show in Vegas. It was on a network station broadcasting across the country. I was feeding our dog, Willy, a toy Yorkie we've had for a number years since before we moved to Vegas from Michigan.

I jumped when I heard an alarm go off. It was a security feature that came with the house we purchased when we first moved to Vegas. I liked the security features of the house and Penny liked the stripper pole planted out by the half-sized Olympic pool out back. The house sat on a lonely road overlooking the Las Vegas valley and the strip of casinos and hotels in the distance. It was also at the foot of one of the mountains that ranged around the valley affording us privacy from the back of our property.

I shut down the alarm, turned on the monitor and saw a postal worker driving away in the truck. I took Willy out for a walk and a dump as I went to the mail box on a post by the road. Willy chased a butterfly while I took the mail out of the box.

"Willy, stop!" I yelled to the dog before he could catch the butterfly. Willy stopped and sat down, looking at me with his dumb expression. "Good puppy," I said and walked back to the house. Willy followed.

At the snack bar I looked over the mail. Mostly junk wanting us to sign up for some credit card or for car insurance. I sorted and tossed the junk. Then, I studied one envelope, a square beige greeting card sized envelope addressed to us with very neat script handwriting. It was stamped with a forwarding address from our old address in Michigan. I was amazed it took almost six months to get to us.

I carefully opened the envelope and pulled a card out. It was an engraved invitation from Penny's and my old high school back in Michigan. It was for a class reunion.

I tried to do the math in my head, I still couldn't. The invite said it was a forty-five year reunion but I felt that was short by a year or two. I wondered if

Penny would want to go back to Michigan to this reunion. The invite said that due to problems, the reunion last year, number forty-five had been canceled. So they were backing up one year.

I smiled. My school always did what they wanted, even changing years. My mind wandered back to just before I met Penny again, after nearly forty years of being away from her. We were in the same school and, although she was a couple years younger than I, she had a really big crush on me. I could never figure out why, but I didn't question it.

My mind also thought about the murders of cheerleaders that took place and Penny was supposed to be one of the victims. That was when Penny and I got back together, much to my delight. We stayed together and then moved out here. Happily ever after. Until I could be murdered by some criminal that I was hired to follow.

My private investigating and security firm was thriving, and going through many changes. I sat at the snack bar and set the invite down. Memories were flooding into my head. Some I'd rather forget. We had a good life in Vegas and my firm was keeping me and my associates busy. Will Trapper and Earl Daws, both retired cops from back home in Michigan, joined me at my firm and we picked up a number of people along the way.

Reunion Murders

Recently, we had a female homicide lieutenant from Vegas LVMPD join our firm. Lynn Carter had retired from the force after she had a baby. My friend, and the cop who saved Penny's life, Deacon DeAngelo, married Lynn and then they had a beautiful baby girl. I could never remember her full name so I just called her PJ, after Penny and me, which was part of her name.

I picked up my cell phone from where I left it on the counter and called Lacey, my office manager and certifiable crazy person. She picked up after two rings. Long enough for her to see the caller ID.

"If you say you aren't coming in, I'll hunt you down," she said briskly.

"I'm coming in. I just wanted to ask if Penny was there."

"She came in about a half hour ago, after she finished her show for the day."

"She's still there?"

"She is. And wondering where you are."

"I'll be there shortly," I said, and hung up.

I gathered up Willy in his travel pouch and headed out to the Crown Vic. I knew Lynn was coming in today to get settled into her office.

Bob Moats

Actually, it was my office, but it was big enough for two people and we had no more available room since Buck took the last space for an office. Buck was settling into his duties as a P.I, since his license came in the mail. He was happy and we kept him busy with small cases for now.

I parked and went in the back door, setting off the cowbell and I waved to the camera. Down the hall, I could see Penny and Lynn talking outside my office door. They both smiled at me as I came up.

"About time you got in. Lynn was ready to throw out all your stuff and take over," Penny said and kissed me on the cheek.

"Morning, Lynn. All moved in I see."

"Yep, ready to start. I applied this morning for my private license, it should be in anytime. Captain Weber wasn't happy that I was leaving the force, but he'll get over it. I feel sorry for Deacon, now alone with Weber. He'll get over it, too. I feel so relaxed being away from the grind of homicide."

"I'll see if we can stir up a murder or two for you," I said with a smile.

"That's all right. I'll take a good embezzlement case, missing person or even follow a cheating spouse."

11

"Oh, I have some mail you might like to see," I said to Penny as I let Willy out of his bag and pulled the invitation from the front pouch, handing it to her.

She opened it and read the card, smiling. "So, we have to go back to Michigan for this?"

"We could fly everyone out here for the thing. But, I don't feel like putting out that much money to see people I hardly knew in high school," I said.

"It would be interesting to go back and see the people we couldn't stand. Maybe I'll see a few friends and we can visit with your family. We haven't seen them in a few years."

"True. This letter was delayed because of our move, so we have one week to get ready to go show off for everyone. Shall I R.S.V.P. our visit?"

"Go ahead. I'm game to show you off now that you're a famous private dick," Penny said laughing.

Lynn said, "Sure, hire me then take off, leaving me alone."

"Don't fret. Jim is hardly in the office anyway. It's almost like you'll be alone a lot," Penny said.

"Hey, I work hard here, too." I defended myself.

Bob Moats

"Can't prove it by me," came a voice behind me, it was Lacey. "And who are you?"

"The person who pays you and can fire you," I said with a grin.

*

Chapter 2

Lacey smiled. "Oh yeah, you're the owner of this place. I almost forgot! You have a person up front who wants to talk to a detective. Do we have any around?"

"No, but we do have private investigators. Does he think he's in a police station?" I asked.

"He looked a little confused. Says he's from the Delta Blues Hotel and Casino. That new one over on Rainbow Boulevard. He's not a happy person."

"You can tell this, how?" I asked.

"He scowled and growled at me. I was ready to call Buck to throw him out, but he told me he wanted to hire us. He's kind of like Angelo; looks like an enforcer for the mob."

"Well, we don't want to keep him waiting then, do we?" I turned to Lynn and said, "Why don't you come along. You may end up taking this case since Earl and Trapper are busy with their own." I said.

She agreed, then I noticed she had her Sig Sauer in a holster on her belt. I smiled and said, pointing to it, "Hard to get away from being a cop?"

"Oh…yeah. I put it on this morning when I was getting ready. Force of habit, I guess. If you don't want me to carry, I can leave it at home."

I pulled back my jacket to show her my Glock. "You know I've always carried this, so I'm fine with you having yours. Penny carries hers in her purse. She won't wear the holster I gave her."

"It makes my clothes bulge around my waist," Penny said, with a smirk.

"Yes, it messes with your perfect figure."

"Better believe it, sweetie," she replied.

"Shall we go see our mob wiseguy?"

We went down the hall through the glass doors to the lobby. At the counter stood a short, thick-necked man in a black suit that didn't fit him well. He did look like a mob figure. I had a number of experiences with the mob in my time as a P.I. and having Angelo as friend kept the mob close by.

Angelo dropped into our lives when Penny and I came to Vegas to get married. He was part of a family from New York and we became friends through numerous interactions over the last number of years. This last year, I helped Angelo open his own restaurant in Vegas and he was a happy ex-mob enforcer. My newly discovered daughter was his head chef, and she was also happy in her job.

"I'm Jim Richards, may I help you?" I asked.

"Yeah, I got word from an old acquaintance of mine, Angelo DeMarco. He said you were good people and could help me." He did growl, but I figured it was just his voice. His face seemed to be molded into a permanent scowl and it made him look rough.

"Yes, Angelo is a good friend of ours. Do you have a problem that requires my attention?"

"It's a small problem. I just need someone to watch one of my people. I think he is skimming money from the casino. I need to know if he is."

"Don't you have security of your own?"

"Yeah, but they're all guards, not undercover types. I need someone who can come in and watch the guy without drawing suspicion."

"What does he do in your casino?"

"He's a cash room supervisor. I could just move him out but I got to answer to my bosses out in Jersey. He's kind of a relative of one of the big bosses - if ya know what I mean."

"I need to ask something off the record. I know Angelo was once with the Traviano Family. I know what their business is and I wonder if your bosses would be in the same kind of business?"

"Yeah, they are a small time mob family. They had some legit money and wanted to invest in a small casino. So they bought the Delta Blues. The gaming commission is keeping an eye on them, but they have been totally business-like. If this mook is skimming, that would be bad for the bosses and their venture."

"How would I be able to put someone in to watch him?" I asked.

"I could hire a new cash room counter and they would be able to keep an eye on him."

I looked back at Lynn and she smiled. "Think you could handle it?"

"Better than watching dead bodies," she said.

I turned back to the man and said, "I'm sorry, I didn't get your name."

"I didn't give it," he said with a grin showing good straight teeth. "I'm Vito Francheta. Good to make your acquaintance, Mr. Richards."

"Okay Mr. Francheta, follow my associate, Ms. DeAngelo. She can get on this for you."

"DeAngelo? Nice Italian name," he said.

"It's my husband's name, his family is Italian. Follow me please." She turned and led the man to our office.

"With Lynn in my office, I don't have anywhere to go to be alone with you now," I said quietly to Penny.

"Lucky for me," she said. "I have to go do some shopping for clothes to go to our reunion."

"You have two huge closets full of clothing. Can't you find something in one of those to wear? I'm sure we'll only be out there for a weekend."

"Yes, there's the reunion at night, but then the picnic is the next day. I have to have some nice outdoor clothes to wear for that." She gave me a kiss and went through the front doors to her car.

"I swear if she dies it will take me months to clean out her closets. I could have a yard sale."

Lacey laughed. "She'll probably want to be buried with her clothes, knowing her."

"True, I'd better buy three cemetery plots, one for me and two for her and her clothes."

I turned and went back to my office, but stopped at the door. Lynn was still arranging things with Francheta. I had the feeling I may need to add on to the building to put more offices in. I'll have to call a building contractor soon.

I went to the back to where Buck had put his office in the old store room. He was at his desk reading some papers, so I knocked on his open door.

"Hey Jimmy, come on in," Buck said, as I sat on his client chair. "I was just filling out this report on the case I was just on. Some husband cheating on his wife and she wants to take him for everything. The dummy signed a pre-nup that gives her everything if he cheats. What's up with you?"

"Well, there's a class reunion back in Michigan and Penny and I are going to it. Do you feel like going back with us to see your family? I could charter a jet to take us."

"Well, thank you Jim. That would be real nice. I haven't seen my brother in over a year. Would be nice to visit."

"I may ask Trapper if he wants to go, too, and see his mother. May as well take everyone."

"Even Earl?"

"If he wants to go, but I don't think he has any family back there. But I'll ask him."

"When do we go?"

"The end of this week, Friday morning. I know its short notice, but I just got the invite today. Took almost six months of mail-forwarding to get here. I'll give you all the details as soon as I can."

Lacey came to the door and said, "Buck, your client is here to get the goods on her husband."

"Thanks, Lacey. I'll be right up."

I stood and said, "Since I'm sharing an office with Lynn for now, I have to let her have her privacy. She has her first client."

"Well, you'll have to add on to the building," Buck said as he headed to the door.

"I was thinking that," I replied as I followed him out of his office. I went back out front, passing Buck and his client. She was a good-looking woman in her thirties, I would say. Her husband was crazy to stray.

I went behind the front counter to where Lacey had her domain set up. She gave me the eye and asked, "What are you doing back here?"

"I need the phone book. I have to find a contractor to add a wing on the building. We need more room." I picked up the phone book from the shelf behind the counter and went to the chair next to Lacey's desk. She was watching me carefully.

"I know a contractor that worked on an addition to the casino I worked at. He was fast and had the job done without disturbing anyone. I could track him down," she said.

"Okay, do that. But get him on this today. I can see sharing an office isn't for me." I stood and put the book back.

Lynn came out the doors to the lobby, followed by her client. She thanked him and he smiled to me as he left the building.

Lynn came over and grinned, "I now work for the Delta Blues Casino."

*

Chapter 3

"I hope you don't have problems working for a mob family. I know that your father did and you have no love for the Mafia," I said.

"That was a long time ago. My dad had no choice. Besides, knowing Angelo has elevated my opinion of the mobs a little. I just tolerate them now. I used to work in a casino years ago, before I became a cop. So I know the routine to do this," Lynn said with a big smile.

"When do you start your new job?"

"Tomorrow. Vito said we had to get on it fast. The Jersey bosses want answers."

"So they are aware of the skimming?" I asked.

"All but the relative of the mook," she said, laughing. "That's a term I haven't heard since I was a child. The relative is big in the family and the bosses don't want to piss him off without proof."

"Well, be careful. I don't want to lose you before we give you your first paycheck," I said.

"Don't worry. I'll be around to spend it. What can I buy with it? A box of chocolates?" she said, laughing.

"Hey, we pay well. At least two boxes of chocolates," I replied, keeping a straight face.

She smiled, shook her head and went back to the office. I turned to Lacey and said, "Get that contractor out here quickly."

I wanted to go into my office but waited until Lynn left. She said she was going home to get ready for her first assignment. I entered my office and sat at my desk. Willy came in after me and sat at my feet. I picked him up and put him on the desk. He plopped down, rested his head and snorted.

I knew I was being silly, but I liked my privacy. Because of the lack of space, I had offered to share my office with Lynn when we first talked about her joining the firm. I didn't think that it would mean giving up my privacy.

I took the reunion invitation from my jacket pocket, looked at it and smiled. I wasn't fond of a good number of people in my class. I hung out more with the underclassmen. Not that there was anything wrong with my fellow classmates, but I just didn't relate to most of them. Penny was in the group of underclassmen I hung with. I had an attraction to her, but I was more hung up on another female and Penny wasn't always on my mind. Besides, she'd had a couple suitors following her around. Too bad I didn't know back then that she was hung up on me.

I heard the doors to the lobby open and close. I wondered who would come down the hallway and waited to see. I figured it was Lacey coming to tell me that she found the contractor, but it was Will Trapper. He gave me a grin when he saw I was looking at him standing outside my door.

"Morning, Jim," he said and came in the room. "How's our newest member doing so far?"

"She's out right now getting ready for her first assignment." I explained what had happened this morning as he sat on my client chair and listened.

"She'll fit right in. How's she taking to her new office?"

"She's doing fine," I replied. "But I wish I could give her a private office,"

"Feeling a little exposed with someone else in your office? Can't fool around with Penny now," he said with a smirk.

"That's part of it, yes." I grinned sheepishly. "I just like being alone in my office once in a while. I can close my door and take a nap if I want to. I have Lacey looking for a contractor to add a wing. That will get Buck out of the store room and give him and Lynn their own offices."

"I felt sorry for Buck when we put him back there. He looks so cramped. An addition will be nice. We could even put in an executive lounge."

"Don't start making this bigger than it needs to be. We're not going to build a huge addition, just offices and maybe a gym. Maybe a lounge, that sounds good. We could put in a pool for Penny to swim so I can admire her in her bikini," I said, looking at the poster of her in the skinny bikini. I had that poster made from a photo I took during our ocean cruise.

Trapper laughed and stood. "I have to make out my report for the case I was just on. Lacey already warned me when I came in. That girl worries too much about reports."

"She feels important and those reports are part of her duties. Make her happy and she gets it done."

"We all know she's important. She actually runs this business in her own small way."

"Yes, she does. Oh, before you go, I have one other thing to tell you. Sit back down."

He did and looked concerned. "Whatcha got?"

I picked up the invitation and handed it to him. "Got this in the mail this morning. Penny and I decided to go back to Michigan to this reunion of my class of 1967. Penny didn't graduate with me. She was two years behind me so this is actually my class reunion."

"Well, this should be fun."

"I asked Buck if he wanted to go back with us to see his family. I'm going to charter a private jet. Do you think you'd like to go too? You could see your mom that way."

Trapper gave me a big smile and said, "Thank you, I'd like that. I'll keep my schedule open for the weekend. Mind if I bring Samantha?"

"Nope, the more the merrier. Since it's a charter we can fill it to capacity. Even with Penny's suitcases."

Trapper laughed, knowing how I always cringed whenever Penny and I took a trip and she packed way too much. "I'll pack light to give her more room."

"Thanks. She's out buying more clothes now for the trip," I said, shaking my head. "Let me know if Sam is coming so I can get an idea on how many people are going. I'm sure Maria won't come with Buck. She'll probably have to work in her show."

"What about Deacon? He's from back there, too," Trapper asked.

"I thought about him. He would have to get time off from the department. He'd probably want to take Lynn if she has her case closed on time. I'll talk to him and see. We could just make a big party of it, couldn't we?"

"Yes, we could." He stood again and headed to the door. "Let me know the details so I can talk to Sam."

"I will," I said, and he left. I stood, took Willy from his nap on the desk and put him on the floor. He followed me out as I headed back up front. Lacey was on the phone as I came to the counter. I stood, waiting for her to finish.

She hung up, then looked up and saw me. She jumped and gave her little scream. "Damn it, will you stop creeping up on me? You know that bugs me."

I was trying not to laugh. Lacey was always in her own little world and was easily surprised. "I'm sorry, force of habit."

"Well, stop it. I just talked to Ben Higgins, the contractor, and he said he'll come out as soon as possible to talk to you about the addition. He said a simple extension would be no problem."

"Trapper and I were talking about a lounge and a gym, maybe a pool too. Of course we'd also have to have offices for Lynn and Buck. I'll see if Ben can handle that."

"Dream on. A gym? What use would you have for that?" she said with a grin.

"I could lose a little of this beer gut with exercise," I replied.

"You could just stop drinking beer, which would help."

"Perish the thought. Now that Lynn has departed, I'm going in my office to meditate," I said and headed to the door.

"Nap, you mean," she said quietly.

"I heard that," I yelled before the door swung shut.

I could hear her laughing as I got to my office, Willy at my heels. I went in and closed the door. The couch was calling my name.

*

Chapter 4

All the people in my firm knew that when my door was closed it meant I didn't want to be disturbed. Everyone except Lynn. She came in and went to her desk before she saw me on the couch.

"Oh, Jim," she said. "I'm sorry. I didn't know you were resting." She was trying not to laugh.

I swung my legs over the side and sat up. "No problem. I was just recharging my batteries."

"You still use batteries? I have solar panels." Now she laughed.

"Funny. What are you doing back here? I thought you were getting ready to work in the morning?"

"I am, but I needed the paper Francheta filled out. I'm ashamed to admit I forgot it. It has all the info I need to start."

"I won't tell anyone that you're absent-minded. Did you have to help him fill it out?"

"No, actually he's pretty smart. We talked a little about his casino. He had good ideas for fixing it up and adding features. Since I worked at a casino I understand the way they operate. He wants to streamline the Delta Blues."

"You should have told him to change the name. Blues may be fine in New Orleans but it's a downer in Vegas. Most gamblers end up with the blues after they lose their paycheck. Why warn them in advance?"

Lynn smiled. "I agree, but that's the name they filed for with the gambling commission. It's a lock on the name. If they would change it, then the commission would get suspicious as to why they want it changed. They're being real careful on how they handle the business until the commission leaves them alone."

"Whatever. I hope you're careful. I think little PJ would miss her mommy if you got rubbed out by the mob."

"PJ? Have you given a nickname to my daughter?"

"Yes, it's easier than saying Penelope Jamie Wilhelmina Earlene Georgina Angel Carter-DeAngelo. I know you named her after all of us, but you and Deacon are nuts."

"Okay. I can see your point. PJ is alright with me. I'm kind of regretting her name. But it's on the birth certificate now."

Lacey came to the door. "Jim, the contractor is here to talk to you." She went back to the front.

"Contractor? What contractor?" Lynn asked.

"I had Lacey call a contractor to see about getting an addition to the building so you and Buck can have decent offices."

She laughed. "You just want to be able to nap without being disturbed."

"Everyone knows not to disturb me, except you."

"Well, I'll leave you to the contractor. I will depart now, the office is yours." She picked up the papers and left.

I stood and went out to the front lobby. The man was tall, lean and good looking. I hoped Penny wouldn't return too soon.

"Mr. Richards, pleasure to meet you. Your secretary was filling me in on what you need."

"Well then, we're done." I turned to Lacey. "Are you also going to pay for the addition?"

Lacey gave me a sheepish smile.

I turned back to the man. "Sorry, I enjoy yanking my office manager's chain. You know who I am, and you are?"

"Ben Higgins." He held his hand out to shake. I took it. "Lacey was saying you need extra room for offices. Good that you are doing well."

"We are doing good, thanks. Yes, I need more offices. So what can you do for us?"

"I have some ideas if you and I could go look around the outside of the building."

"Sure. Lacey, hold my calls."

Lacey grinned. "What calls?"

"You can be replaced," I said and took Higgins outside. We spent about a half hour talking and he gave me some ideas. Ones I liked. I hired him after he gave me a cost.

"Can you guarantee that price?"

"I'll hold myself to it. My company can use the work right now. Building trades are slow in Vegas. The economy is picking up slowly but not fast enough. I'll hold to my price."

"When can you start?"

"I have my men on standby." He grinned and I held my hand out. We shook on it. "I'll have my crew here in the morning. I'll have to go get the building permits today. I know a few people in the city who can push it through."

"Fine, start it." He said he would and left. I was standing looking at the building when I felt someone standing behind me. I was ready to pull my Glock when I heard a familiar voice. It was Penny.

"Why are you standing there staring at the building?" she asked.

"I'm having an addition put on this side. A couple offices for Buck and Lynn. Maybe a lounge, too."

"Lounge? You're hardly in the building long enough to use a lounge."

"Whatever. Lacey and Tracey can use it. Maybe Earl and Trapper will get use of it. Did you find clothes for our trip?"

"Of course I did. I'm good to go. How long will we be out there?"

"I figure leaving Friday morning and staying until Monday. We'll have the weekend to visit family and attend the reunion. Oh, Buck, Trapper and Sam are also going so far. I'm going to see if Deacon and Earl want to go. Lynn will probably have to stay back here. Besides her case, I'll let her run the office for the experience. The baby may be too young to travel."

"I'll talk to Lynn. Maybe we can see if she can go. Lacey can run the office. Have you chartered a plane yet?"

"Plane? No, I chartered a jet just before I rested in my office. It will be ready Friday morning at the same private terminal that Angelo's mother came in at."

"Good, it will be nice not having to deal with commercial airlines."

"Yep, I'll be sure they have a nice meal prepared too."

"What's the movie?"

"Movie? I hadn't thought about a movie. I guess I'll have to get that movie about the pilot who brings in his plane upside-down."

"Or you could get 'Airplane' and we can get a laugh out of it."

My cell phone buzzed and I took it out. The caller ID said it was Deacon. "Hey, big guy, what's up?"

I put it on speaker so Penny could hear.

"I was just checking to see how Lynn was doing. Do you have her sitting on a stakeout for a cheating spouse?"

"Nope, she's got her first case to watch a casino manager and see if he's skimming funds. She starts in the morning. I forgot to ask Lynn, who's watching the baby?"

"We hired Earl's girlfriend, Paula. She volunteered and we took her up on it."

"That should make Earl happy. Having a baby around. I haven't seen him today to ask."

"When Lynn talked to Paula, she said Earl was good with it. He'll probably hang out more at the office now."

I looked at Penny and said quietly, "See? A lounge will come in handy."

Penny gave me one of her famous I-give-up looks and went to the front of the building, leaving me standing in the field alone. I took Deacon off speaker.

"How's Weber holding up without Lynn around?"

"He's doing okay so far. He keeps coming by to check on me, so he's starting to bug me. I need a case to get out of the office."

"I'm sure one will pop up. While we're on the subject of getting out of the office, Penny and I are going back to Michigan next weekend for a class reunion. Do you want to go? It's just for four days."

"Class reunion? How many years?"

"Forty-six on last count, but they're calling it forty-five because they didn't have it last year. Buck and Trapper agreed to go. I chartered a jet to fly us back. See about Lynn and if she'd want to go."

"I'll ask, but with the baby and her new job, she may opt to stay. I'd like to visit a few relatives still there."

"Well, let me know so I can take a head count."

"Okay, I have to go. I see Weber heading my way. Talk later." He hung up and I put my cell away.

I took one last look at the building and went back in. Tracey was at her desk in the front lobby looking bored.

"I'm going to get you a small TV you can watch while you wait out here."

"That would be nice. I've gotten tired of reading."

"Take some money out of petty cash and go get one of those small TVs. Nothing too big. Just pick one out that you'd like."

"Thanks, I appreciate it," she said as I went into the main lobby. Penny was at the counter talking to Lacey.

"What are you two plotting?"

"We were talking about the new addition. We are thinking of ways to decorate the lounge," Penny said with her evil grin.

Great, I thought. There goes our man cave.

*

Chapter 5

"Don't add anything until the addition is built. Okay?"

Penny smiled and came to me. "Sorry, sweetie. We'll go easy on your hideaway. Just a few frilly curtains and doilies on the tables."

"You are an evil woman. I'm going to my office and I don't want to be disturbed. Especially by you."

I went through the doors to my office and saw Earl coming in the back door. I waited for him to approach, but he went into his office. I felt slighted so I went down the hall to his door.

"Did you not see me?" I asked.

"Yes, I saw you. Did you want to talk to me?"

"Well, I had something to ask you. Penny and I are going back to Michigan for my class reunion. I'm chartering a commercial jet. Are you interested in going with us?"

"Who else is going?"

"So far Buck, Trapper and Deacon. I don't have commitments from the women yet."

"If Lynn isn't going, Paula won't go. She's watching Lynn and Deacon's baby. If Lynn doesn't go, will Deacon stay? If Maria doesn't go, will Buck want to go? The logistics of this will be tough. Good luck."

"I'll work it out. Let me know if you want to go. I know you don't have family back there so I'll understand if you don't."

"Thanks. I left Michigan for a reason and I don't really want to go back. Even for a visit."

"Don't you want to go see all the men in your old precinct? Just to see how they turned out?

He was quiet for a moment. "I've thought about them. I left the force kind of abruptly. It may be nice to see some of the ones I liked. I'll let you know."

"By Wednesday, please. So I can get a head count."

I left his office more confused than when I started the project. I might just take Penny and go out to Michigan, leaving everyone here. I entered my office and found Willy stretched out on my chair. I had no idea how he got up there. Sometimes he amazes me. I picked him up and put him on the desk. He plopped back down and closed his eyes. I wanted to close mine too, so I sat in my desk chair, lay back and tried to nod off.

My door opened and in came Penny. I gave up. "What part of don't disturb don't you understand?"

"Sweetie, you know that doesn't pertain to me. I'm hungry. Shall we go eat?"

"Call for a pizza. Enough for everyone and have it delivered."

"You're getting to be an old poop. I think you need vitamins."

"I need to have less stress."

"I'm not stressing you, am I?"

I leaned forward in my chair and said, "No, babe. You're not. It's everything else. I think we may drive back to Michigan in the van. Let the others who want to go take the jet. We can leave Tuesday. It took me and my son three days to drive to Michigan, so you and I could relax on the way."

"I'm not going to be able to take time off from my show for you to play explorer."

"Crap, I forgot about that. You're taking off Friday and Monday, right?"

"Yes, I told Gordy and they are going to run previous shows. I want to fly back to Michigan with a nice dinner and a movie. I had enough roughing it when we went to Seattle."

"Okay, then you organize everyone who may go with us. It's now your job to be social director."

"Fine. Now I'm still hungry and I don't want pizza."

I stood, picked up Willy and took Penny out to the lobby. "Lacey, order a pizza for you, Tracey and anyone else in the building. Get a couple so we can have leftovers."

She gave me a grin and went to her phone book. I told her Penny and I were leaving and we went out to Penny's car.

We went to have a nice meal at Angelo's restaurant. Unfortunately both Angelo and my daughter were off work that day. We still enjoyed our meal and then went home to relax. Penny decided to take a dip in the pool and I went for a walk with Willy down the road. I thought that Willy wasn't getting enough exercise and was sleeping too much. We went for about a half mile then turned around and came back home. There was a car in the drive when Willy and I arrived. It was Lynn's car.

I led Willy to the front door and we went in. Penny, Lynn and Deacon were sitting in the front room. Willy made a bee line to Penny and she picked him up.

"Did Daddy take you for a long walk?"

"He walked me," I said, then greeted our guests. "So what brings you here to our humble abode?"

Lynn spoke first. "Well, my assignment to watch the embezzling manager is on hold. It seems he was murdered today."

I sank into a chair, surprised. "What happened?"

Deacon said, "We got a call from the Delta Blues that there was a situation. It seems one of their managers was murdered this morning. It was the man Lynn was supposed to watch. I arrived and found the man in a storeroom, dead. CSI did a sweep on the room, but it was used by everyone in housekeeping so there was plenty of trace from about a dozen people. Lynn told me he was the person she was supposed to watch for embezzling. So we're wondering if it could be someone higher up who did him in or had him done in."

"I think they may have been trying to protect their investment in the casino by getting rid of one bad apple," Lynn said.

"But wouldn't this bring in the gambling commission to investigate also?" I asked.

"That's what I thought. But they are leaving it up to LVMPD and we have to file a report after we solve this. Weber asked Lynn to give us a hand with the case."

"I wasn't sure if I should agree, but since you always interfered in our cases, I said yes."

"Interfere?" I said. "You guys couldn't solve half your cases without me."

"No big head here. Since you are leaving the city, we have to go this alone," Lynn said. "I'm so sad."

"So I guess you and Deacon won't be going on our trip back to Michigan with us?"

"Michigan? What trip?" Lynn asked.

I looked at Deacon. "You haven't told her about it?"

"Didn't see any reason to since we are both on the case now." He looked at Lynn and said, "I'll explain later."

S

"So are you going to get paid for this?" I asked.

"Well, I called Vito and he asked me to find out who did the kill. So I'm still on the case but with a different direction. I get paid to work with the cops, only my pay is better." She grinned and pushed her elbow into Deacon.

"Has Weber agreed to this?"

"It was his idea. He asked me to ask Lynn to help out. So I asked and she agreed."

"Well, if you can solve the case before Friday, you can still go back to Michigan with us."

"There's that Michigan thing again," Lynn said.

"I said I'll explain it to you later," Deacon replied.

"Where's PJ?" Penny asked.

"Paula has her. We're going to get her when we leave here," Lynn said. "Earl is working at the office tonight. I think he just doesn't want to go home. PJ is teething so she's crabby."

We talked a short while but Lynn was getting antsy to pick up her daughter. They said their good-nights and left.

"I doubt they will solve this before we go back to Michigan," Penny said.

"Never can tell. Lynn is good at her job. I'm glad we have her now. I'm wearing down and will be retiring now."

"You're always retiring. When do you plan on actually retiring?"

"Retiring as in sleeping or leaving the work type of retiring?"

"Leaving the firm."

"I'll retire from the firm when you retire from your show. Think that will be anytime soon?"

"Are you kidding? I just got my network show back. My fans would kill me if I retired now."

"Fine, I'm retiring for the night then. You can do that can't you?"

"Yes, if you don't attack me in bed."

"Me? Never. You're safe to go to sleep if you want."

"I didn't say I would go to sleep. You can have your way with me tonight. But for only the next half hour, so move on it." She stood and went to the bedroom. I followed.

*

Chapter 6

Early next morning, Penny went off to tape her show, taking Willy with her. I dug through my closet to see what clothes I had to take on our trip. I wasn't a clothes-horse, so I didn't have much to worry about. I pulled my suitcase from the bottom of the closet and started to pack a few things that I wouldn't need during the rest of the week. I was finally satisfied with my selections and closed the case.

I went out to the kitchen for my morning toast and then thought I would go to the precinct to visit Lynn and Deacon. I had a feeling Lynn would end up back there helping with a case or two. Unfortunately, that meant they wouldn't need me. Now I really had to do some work for the firm.

I drove out to LVMPD, enjoying the sunshine. It was hot so my air was on full blast. I pulled in and parked then went into the building. The desk officer at the back door greeted me and waved me through. Deacon was in Lynn's old office. Lynn wasn't there.

"Hey, big guy, where's the little woman?"

Deacon grinned and pointed behind me. I turned and saw that Lynn must have followed me and was giving me a look. "Little woman? I hope you'll never use that term again."

"Sorry, I'll refrain from using it. So what's going on?"

Lynn went into the office and sat, motioning me to sit. I did.

"The mook," she said with a grin, "was found dead early yesterday by a maid. The management called the police and Deacon got the lead. I'll let him tell you the rest."

Deacon cleared his throat and said, "I went there and found the victim inside a clothes hamper. According to Joe Lang he had been stabbed. Joe took the body back to the morgue and will let me know what he determines, but it looks like he was killed by a stab from some sharp weapon. "

"Stabbing? Did it look like a hit on him? Maybe the mob wanted him out of the way."

Lynn said, "The mob likes to take their victims out to the desert and drop them off. Make them disappear. They don't usually leave them in the hotel with people around to find the body."

Deacon added, "The supply room where he was found wasn't the main scene of the stabbing. Not enough blood found. He was murdered elsewhere and dumped in the room. Probably brought in by the clothes hamper. CSI has finished with the crime scene and will get back with me if they come up with something. I got Warren going through the surveillance videos to see if he can find anything."

"So, Jim, Deacon tells me you have a big reunion to go to this weekend."

"Yep, my forty-fifth. Well, forty-six actually. They didn't celebrate last year. I don't suppose you two can go?"

"Unless we find the killer in two days, no. Deacon has no real family left out there. His sister lives here, and I'm from here so I have no family there. I doubt we'll be able to go, but thanks for the offer."

"Trapper is going back to see his mother, and taking Sam. Buck has a couple brothers to visit. Don't know yet if Maria is going. So my guest list is dwindling. Not that it's necessary that everyone goes, just makes it fun that way."

Reunion Murders

"Sorry to miss the party this time. Maybe when Penny's reunion comes up we'll go," Lynn said.

"That should be next year, if we get the invitation in time. Well, you two have work to do. I have to go to the office and see if they have started the addition on the building for your office."

"Make sure it's as big as yours," Lynn said with a big grin. "I may need to bring in a large couch to rest on."

"You'll get what you get. Don't work too hard," I said and went out. I got into my Crown Vic and drove to the office. The front parking lot had a number of trucks and men moving equipment from the trucks. I parked away from the activities.

Ben Higgins saw me and came over before I got into the building. "Hey, Jim, I got the permits and we are ready to build. I have some blueprints from a similar job so I'll just use those."

"Great. How long do you think the job will go?"

"My men are fast but good. I figure by the beginning of next week. We still have to get the electrical and plumbing installed but it shouldn't delay us too much. It will be up to you how you fix up the interior, carpets and furnishings."

"My wife will handle that. I'm afraid of what she will do."

"I understand. My wife loves to decorate with feminine things. I cringe too."

"Okay, I'll let you get back to work. I have an office to run." We said our good-byes and I went in. I could hear but couldn't see the TV that Tracey had on the back of the counter she sat at.

"Got one, eh?"

"Yes, it's small but functional and has a radio for when there's nothing on TV."

"Good, I don't want you bored out here. You'll have to watch Penny's show too."

"I plan on it. I usually tape it to watch when I get home, but now I can see it here."

"Great," I said and went into the inner lobby. Lacey wasn't at her desk and I wondered where she was. I went up to the counter just as Lacey popped up from behind it and loudly yelled, "Boo!" I about had a heart attack as she laughed.

"See how it feels," she said and went back to her desk.

"You'll regret that, but I understand your point."

"You've been scaring me for a couple years now. I just got my revenge."

"Fine. I hope you're happy. I just left Lynn and Deacon. They have a murder case to solve from the Delta Blues."

"Not the mob wiseguy who came in here to hire us."

"No, it was Lynn's suspect. He turned up dead before she could watch him."

"Is she still on the case?"

"Francheta told her to find the killer so she's still working for the mob."

"Make sure she turns in her reports."

I stared at her, shook my head and went to my office.

It was nice and quiet in the building until the construction started. The addition was going to be on my side of the building, just behind my windows to the outside.

I went to the window and looked out. They were digging a foundation hole and had a cement truck ready to fill. Luckily I had bought the vacant lot next to my property so they had plenty of room to park their equipment. I heard a voice at my door and turned to see Buck.

"I'm anxiously waiting for my new office," he said.

"The contractor said next week. So start thinking about how you are going to decorate before Penny and Lacey take over."

"I'm a simple man. I don't need much. Just office furniture and a couple file cabinets. Maybe some plants, too."

"Make sure they are fake. I didn't ask if there will be windows. I'm sure there will be. Plants need light."

"I work better with fake plants. I'm not good at taking care of them. So what time are we leaving Friday?"

"In the morning, around eight. We're not rushed for time but I want to get going as soon as possible. Is Maria going with us?"

"I talked to her last night and she can't get away. Too many of the dancers are coming up with the flu."

"Flu? I thought we were past that plague."

"Nope. Maria is trying not to get it herself. So I'll be going stag with you guys. Are we meeting here?"

"Yep, that'll work. I'll bring the mini-limo and we can go to the airport in that. Trapper is going and he'll ask Sam if she wants to go. Lynn and Deacon pulled a murder and probably won't make it."

"Trapper and me. We can have fun. I have to go give my finished report to Lacey before she hunts me down. That girl is too wrapped up with these reports."

"She doesn't have a lot else to do. So make her happy."

Buck left and I looked out the window again. They were pouring the cement. I thought about how many people were buried in concrete from a mob hit. I'd have to watch closely to be sure they didn't dump a body.

*

Chapter 7

Two-thousand-twenty-six miles east of Las Vegas a man was hobbling upstairs from the locked room he had in his basement. He carried the well-worn photo of people from his class of forty-six years ago, determined to meet with them during the reunion in a few days. The man's mother came into the kitchen as the man exited from the stairwell.

"What the hell do you do down there, you idiot?" the woman yelled at the man.

"Leave me alone. It's none of your business!" the man yelled back and headed to the back door.

"Where the hell are you going, you little dipshit?"

"None of your business!" he yelled. "Leave me alone!"

He opened the door.

"You go out that door, don't come back!"

Reunion Murders

"If I don't come back, who'll take care of you? Make your food, clean up your messes. You can't function without me, old woman."

"I can live just fine without you. Go away!"

"Why do we always have to go through this every stinking time I go out? Go back to your room and die!" He went out, slamming the door.

"And don't come back!" the woman yelled.

As the man walked away from the door, he said quietly to himself, "In a few days, you won't have to worry about me, you old hag. I'll exact my revenge on you and the people who screwed with me."

~~*~~

I watched for the next two days while they built the addition to the building. Well, I wasn't always there for the two days but when I was, I watched them. Sometimes I'd go outside into the heat of the day and watch them, then retreat back to my office to watch out my window in the air conditioning.

It was Thursday afternoon and I was sitting by the window in my desk chair watching the men struggle in the heat. I admired them for their perseverance and wanting to meet their deadline.

I heard the doors to the front open and close and made a guess as to who was coming down the hall. I was right. It was Penny.

"Are you still watching them? I'm glad you don't have better things to do like solve a murder."

I rolled my chair back to my desk and smiled. "Lynn and Deacon can handle the murders now although I think I may miss helping them. I don't want to step on Lynn's toes since she is working here now. So I'll have to either retire or actually take a case of following a spouse."

"Horrors!" she exclaimed as she mimicked terror. "That would be a fate worse than actually working. You know your books are selling well and you make enough money from them to retire. You're not a spring chicken anymore."

"I feel as old as my mind lets me."

"But your body is as old as the moon."

"I can still function."

"You have been slowing down in the sack, I have to say."

"I'm just going easy on your old body. Now have you eaten?"

"No, how about some tacos? Haven't had them in a while."

"Okay Del Taco it is. Find Willy, he's hiding on me."

Penny went back out front since she had seen Willy by Lacey's desk. Willy came when she called him. I came out behind her and said to Lacey, "We leave in the morning. You're not going to miss me, are you?"

I could tell she was holding in a laugh.

"Of course I will. Who will keep guard over the construction workers?"

"You two are a riot. We're going out to get heartburn. I shall return next week."

"I'll hold my breath," was all I heard from Lacey as we left.

We had our tacos. Willy refused to eat them so we went home. Penny gave him his kibble and I went to my home office computer to check on our flight. The company that I leased the jet from had its schedule posted and I found our flight was going to be on time.

I went out and told Penny then went back to my office to call Trapper.

"Hey, Will, you still going with us?" I said when he answered.

"Yep, I talked to Sam but she can't come. Business or some sort of commitment. I don't know what, but I'm game to go."

"Meet us at our house by 7:30 in the morning. The flight is scheduled for eight."

"Okay, I'll see you then. Oh, I called Barry Becker and he's going to meet us when we arrive."

"That's great. I figured on calling a car service but Barry will be good. How is he doing?"

"Upset that I haven't kept in touch. But he got over it. I'll see you in the morning." He hung up without saying good-bye again.

I sat back in my chair and looked over to the door as Penny walked in.

"Who all is going?"

"Well, so far Trapper, alone. Sam has commitments so she's not going. I haven't called Buck or Earl yet. I'll let you know."

"I'm not worried about who's going. I just want to get back there. Just us or with a wild bunch."

I laughed and said, "Why do you want to get back there?"

"To see your family. I lost my parents after I was a teen so your family is mine now. I may even look up a few of my friends from school while you go reminisce with your peeps."

"Most of my peeps were in your class. I'll have more fun when your class reunion comes up next year."

"Fine, but you better not hook up with any old girlfriends."

"The only girlfriend I had was murdered, if you remember. The other cheerleaders that were killed had nothing to do with me. Other than you. What ever happened to that cheerleader outfit you were going to get and wear?"

"I'm saving it for a special occasion."

"What do you deem as a special occasion?"

"When you make your second million selling your books."

"What, so you can cheer as you murder me for my money?"

"I'll be filthy rich and I can retire to an island in the Caribbean."

I thought on that and said, "We could retire now and move to the Caribbean."

She smiled and said, "I'd prefer to move to the Caribbean by myself. With all that money I could live very well. Cabana boys and massages every day." She grinned and left the room.

Sometimes I wondered about her.

~~*~~

The man hobbled down the stairs to his locked room. He entered and dropped the brown paper bag on his desk. He turned on the desk light and poured out the contents of the bag. He looked over the objects on the desk as he tossed the bag aside. There were nylon ropes, duct tape, and a box of straight pins.

He went to the cork wall and turned the overhead light on. It illuminated the board and he reached for one photo. It was a yearbook photo of a woman. She was good-looking for being about seventeen years old. The hairdo of the times was high on her head. It looked like she was going to the prom. This woman had been in the class hierarchy, well-liked by everyone and with all the trappings of money.

The man brought his face close to the picture and said quietly, "Now, Neena, you are no longer a class princess. I'll take you off your throne and make you beg for mercy."

He turned his head to another yearbook picture of a young man and said, "You too, Ken. I'll make you regret ever treating me like you did that night when you, Neena and Donny made a fool of me."

He heard a noise by the door and turned to see his mother entering.

"I told you never to come in here!" he screamed at her.

"What kind of evil are you doing in here? This is my house! You can't do your evil in my house! What are all those pictures on the wall?"

"None of your damn business! Get out now or so help me, you'll regret it!"

She moved closer and screamed. "You'll do what, you gimp? Will you beat me up? You'll move out? So go get out, you damn cripple!"

Enraged, the man grabbed one of the knives from the table and plunged it into her. He pulled it out and plunged it again. The woman had a shocked look on her face as he pushed her back. She fell to the floor making guttural sounds just before she died. He wiped the knife on his shirt and smiled. "One down, three to go."

*

Chapter 8

At seven in the morning while Penny was still packing I set my two suitcases by the front door to go out to the mini-limo. I figured she'd have at least six or seven suitcases. The woman loved to pack.

I had talked to Buck and Will and they both said they would be there by 7:30. I hoped they would be on time. Willy was bouncing around as I put his travel cage by my stuff. He was good on an aircraft, and he didn't mind being in the cage. Once we were in the air, I would let him out and he would explore.

Penny called from the bedroom; I figured she had finished packing. I went to see what she had and was surprised.

"I see only four cases. Do you have more elsewhere?"

"No, I packed light this time. I know you get flustered when I take too much luggage, so I economized by taking only what I would need. Where are we staying while we're out there?"

"Your house is still there even though we let my son and his family live in it to keep an eye on it. I know my son wouldn't have a problem with us moving back in, but I decided that we need a change of scenery and reserved a room at one of the nicer hotels in the area."

"Do they have a hot tub?"

"I didn't think to ask. We'll see when we get there. Maybe we can change rooms to get one."

I heard the driveway alarm go off.

"Someone's arrived. I'll see who it is." I grabbed two suitcases, went to the living room and saw out the window that Trapper had arrived. He had Buck with him and they were taking luggage out of Trapper's Jeep. I went out to them.

"Where's the limo?" Trapper asked.

"I'll bring it out," I said and went to the garage. I keyed in the passcode to open the door and brought out the car. I parked in front of the house and opened the trunk.

We spent a few minutes putting the luggage in the car. Penny brought out the last two she had and greeted the men.

"G'morning, Penny," Buck said, grinning.

"Morning, Buck, Will. Are you two ready to go?"

They agreed and finished putting the luggage in the car. We all piled in and I drove to the airport. The jet was sweet and sleek. I did good leasing that baby. We loaded our things on the jet and boarded.

The take-off was smooth, as was the flight. I had called ahead to get a dinner for Penny and the others and managed to get an in-flight movie, "Airplane," which we laughed all the way through.

The movie eased the flight across the country. It took about three hours, which went by fast. We touched down at Detroit City Airport and got off the plane.

"Will!" came a familiar voice from a large van. It was Barry Becker and he had a prisoner transport van. Barry was a patrol cop back during the classmate murders. Trapper took him under his wing and taught him to be a decent detective.

"Becker!" Trapper yelled back as the young man came up. They hugged quickly and broke off. "You couldn't get a better vehicle to pick us up in?"

"Sorry, it was the largest one I could get to take everyone in."

We all said our hellos to him and started to remove the luggage from the jet. I thought it was funny to see Buck get into the back of the prisoner transport van. He wasn't happy about it but yielded.

Trapper and I sat near the front and talked to Barry through the cage mesh.

"So is everything still the same at the precinct?" Trapper asked Becker.

"Nothing much has changed. Still the same as when you worked there. Although I'm now a sergeant."

"Well, that's great, Barry. You deserve it," Trapper said. "Are you still in homicide?"

"Sure am. We pulled a case yesterday of an old woman who was stabbed twice and dumped in a garbage container. Sanitation workers found her and we're investigating. The son reported her missing and we're questioning him today. He's from your hometown, Jim."

"Really? What's his name?"

"Mark Jonsen."

It took me a minute to pull the name from my memory cells, then it hit me. "Yes, I knew him. He was in my class and he was a jerk. He was always picking on me and other less macho guys. He wasn't macho, but he was big and mean."

"Well, he's still big, but he hasn't shown us that he's mean. He's been very cooperative and he has sort of an alibi for the presumed time of death."

"Sort of?" Trapper asked.

"He was at a movie double feature in Royal Oak. He had tickets, but no one to identify him. It would be nice if we had the surveillance cameras around here like they do in Vegas."

"Yes, they do help," I said. "Do you see him as a prime suspect?"

"We always suspect family members so we're watching him. Not much else for evidence so far. He's been released, but we're keeping an eye on him."

"I have no qualms thinking of him as the murderer. He was not a good person," I said.

"He tortured you, didn't he?" Trapper said with a smile.

"Let's just say I stayed out of his way."

"Just like you to hide from conflict," Penny said, sitting next to me. "He probably was just misunderstood."

"You weren't in my class to see this guy. He was not well-liked. I remember one night at a school dance in the gym, a girl managed to get him out on the dance floor and two guys panted him. Right in the middle of the dance floor, they pulled down his pants and he didn't have any underwear on. He was so embarrassed he went into a rage. Took three teachers to subdue him and take him out of the gym. He was booted from school for a week, and the others who pulled the stunt on him weren't even scolded. He wasn't the same after that."

"I seem to remember that. It was the talk of the school for a week. I felt sorry for him."

Buck said, "You'd feel sorry for serial killers."

"Buck, if you started murdering people, I wouldn't feel sorry for you," she replied.

"Penny, you hurt my feelings. You can sympathize with Jim's bully, but you wouldn't feel sorry for me."

"Buck, I know you are intelligent and a sweetheart, so if you started murdering people then something would have to be wrong with you. Jim's classmate was a miserable person but he was wronged by a few bad students. It can hurt for a long time."

I said, "Nevertheless, Mark was a bully and an asshole. If he murdered his mother, he deserves to spend time in prison. I'll be watching for him at the reunion."

Becker interrupted. "I'm sorry, where are we going?"

"Barry, take Penny and me to the Holiday Inn Suites on Masonic and Little Mack, then Trapper can direct you to where he needs to go. Buck is going to his brother's home, so you have some traveling to do. Thanks."

Trapper said, "I need to go to my mother's home. I called her over the weekend and she has a room for me."

Reunion Murders

"We'll all meet up at our hotel room tonight to celebrate our arrival, then go our own ways to visit family," I said.

We arrived at the hotel and Penny and I got out of the van. A few heads turned when they saw it was a police transport van dropping off guests. I thought it was hilarious. Barry drove Trapper and Buck to their destinations as we went to check in. I asked if the room had a hot tub and was told all of the rooms that had Jacuzzi's were occupied. He did say there was a Jacuzzi in the pool room on the first floor. Penny liked hearing that there was a pool, so she was happy.

We went up to our room on the top floor. I liked having a good view of the city. Unfortunately, the view was of shopping centers and a mall. But it looked good to be back home. I had arranged for a car rental and it was supposed to be waiting for us at the front when we were ready. I had it delivered.

Penny disappeared into the bathroom and came out in her bathing suit. Not a bikini, but a nice two-piece.

"I'll be by the pool with Willy. You can join us if you promise to be good." She left the room and I decided to rest. I had missed my nap time.

Chapter 9

I was dreaming that I was in a rain storm when I opened my eyes to see Willy on the couch with me. He was shaking water from his fur all over me. Penny was standing above us laughing.

"You're a mean woman," I mumbled, lifting Willy so I could sit up.

"I didn't want to yell and frighten you. You might have had a heart attack and I'd have to waste my weekend trying to bury you."

"You could just call my brother and he'd come over to get my lifeless body. But you'd have to tell my mother that you killed me," I said.

"I'll let you live until we get back to Vegas. I'm hungry. Shall we go eat?" she said as she started to slip out of her wet swim suit.

"If you do that here I may have to ravish your naked body."

Reunion Murders

She looked at me and then went to the other room. I put Willy on the floor and he finished shaking the water.

"How was your swim?" I yelled to her.

"We were doing fine until some man came along and said they didn't allow animals in the pool. I told him that Willy was my son, but he didn't buy that. I didn't have Willy's leash to tie him down, so I came back here," she called back.

"I'll baby sit Willy next time you want to swim. What kind of food do you want?"

"A nice sit-down dinner in a nice restaurant."

"I know one." I stood and went to change clothes.

About a half hour later we were ready. I put Willy in his doggy purse and we went down to find our rental car. The people at the front desk told me it was parked near the front. They gave me the keys the rental people left and we went out. The car was a nice Cadillac SUV, just like I requested.

I drove us over to Mr. Paul's on Groesbeck Highway and parked. I had never eaten there in all the years I lived only five miles from the place, but I knew of their reputation.

Once we were seated I called Trapper and told him what room we were in at the hotel.

"I have my mother's car," he said. "She's renting it to me. She always was an enterprising woman." Trapper laughed. "What time do you want us to come by?"

"We're eating now, so make it about six. That will give us enough time to organize."

"Okay. Do you want me to pick up Buck?"

"If you would. I don't know what his arrangement is. Call him and see," I said.

"Okay, I'll let you know what is going on. See you later." He hung up.

I told Penny what he said and then we ordered our food.

~~*~~

"Damn," Jonsen thought. "I should have buried the old bitch instead of dumping her."

Reunion Murders

He went to the front window and peeked carefully through the curtains. He could see the unmarked police car sitting down the street. He went to his room in the basement and packed all the things he would need into a gym bag. He was ready to do his deed. He took the bag up the stairs to the old Chevy in the attached garage. At least the cops couldn't see what he was doing. He hoped they wouldn't follow him everywhere he went, especially to the reunion tomorrow night. He had a job to do and didn't need interference from anyone.

He went back in the house and picked up the yearbook from the kitchen table. He took it to the living room where his mother had never liked him to relax. He loved the freedom he had now that she was gone. He sat in her favorite easy chair, relishing the comfort that she had denied him.

He opened the book and thumbed through it, looking at all the people he hated back forty-six years ago. Maybe he'd set fire to the place where they were having the reunion, trapping them inside. That would be nice, but he had only three people he really wanted to deal with. He closed the book and put his head back, thinking of the years he had waited until they would all be together again. It was going to be a good night.

~~*~~

Everyone met at the hotel at six and we sat enjoying conversation and drink. We invited Barry Becker to join us.

"So, you got together with your brothers, Buck?" I asked him.

"Yeah, it was good to see them again. You going to visit your family tomorrow?" Buck asked back.

"Yes. I called my brother and he's going to have everyone together at my mother's house. It'll be a nice visit. Then we have to get ready for the reunion tomorrow night. I'm not crazy about seeing a number of those people, but it'll be interesting."

"Most of the classmates I associated with are either dead or in jail." Buck laughed.

"I may have arrested a few of them myself," Trapper said.

"Very true. So, Jim, you have one former classmate involved in murder. You think he'll ask you to solve the crime?" Buck asked.

"I hope not. I never cared for him back then. I don't think I'll like him now."

"You'll probably hide from him at the reunion," Penny said.

"I will not. I'm a big time P.I. now, and I'll stand up to him."

"So you're taking your Glock?" Penny smiled.

"You betcha."

"Do you want police protection?" Becker asked me with a smile.

"No, Barry, I think I can handle it. I won't let him bully me again. Besides, I have Penny to protect me."

"Better believe he won't get near you while I'm around." She mugged a tough face.

We talked until about eleven and I told everyone to go so we could get some sleep. They all left and Penny went to the bedroom to change into her pajamas. I came in and got undressed then climbed into the big king-size bed. Willy was at our feet sleeping peacefully. Penny nestled under my arm and sighed.

"What?" I asked.

"Just happy. Our lives are enriched by our friends and our surroundings. I even like you."

"I hope so."

"Just don't get involved in any murders. You have Trapper here. He can handle it."

"True, and don't forget Buck. He's now licensed to investigate. I can relax over the weekend."

"You'd better," she said and snuggled close.

The next morning, the sun was coming in our window and the alarm in my android phone was playing my wake-up tune. I shut off the alarm and got up. Willy and Penny were not in the room. I found a note saying that she was going for a morning swim and she took the leash for Willy. I went to the window and looked out. It was going to be a nice day, blue skies and sunshine. Not the way I remembered gloomy, grey Michigan. One thing about Vegas, it's always sunny.

A half hour later, Penny came back and we got ready to go visit my family. We went to the rental car again and drove over to my mother's house. Everyone was there. We had a nice time visiting and it was good to see everyone again.

We visited until four then said we had to go get ready for the reunion. I told my mother that we would come back after the picnic the next day. My son and his little family said they would come back also. We had a flight out from City Airport at eight in the morning on Monday, so we'd have one more chance to visit Sunday night.

Penny and I said our good-byes and headed back to the hotel.

"It was nice to see the family again," Penny said on the way. "I do miss them. You have good relatives, sweetie."

"I come from good genes. The family is talented and loves to be self-employed. My brother makes good money as a photographer, and my dad, before he passed away, had his own woodworking shop. Us Richards are independent."

"But you have me to boost you up in your business," she said.

"Yes, I don't know how many times you have saved the day by catching the killers with your gun or a heavy lead pipe. Let's not forget the fire extinguisher."

"It's been seven times. I kept count. I should be paid for my actions."

"You can take it out in trade," I said.

"I hope you're not talking sex. That would be like no pay at all." She grinned and stifled a laugh.

Chapter 10

We had a little time before the reunion so we relaxed in the room. I called Buck to see what he had been up to and he said he was happy visiting his family.

"Jimmy, my brothers and I have been working on their classic Mustang. We've been working on souping up the engine. It's a cherry machine. How did your visit with your family go? How's your mom?"

"She's good, everyone is good. Nice to see them again. Are you going to work on cars tomorrow?"

"I'm not sure. It's Sunday and the family is going to church. I'm probably going to stay home. I never got into the Holy Roller thing. They're born again. I'm not."

I glanced at Penny and said to Buck, "You're more than welcome to come with us to the picnic."

Penny laughed and said quietly, "You just want a bodyguard." I gave her the finger which made her laugh even more.

"Is that proper? I didn't graduate from your school," Buck said.

"I'm allowed to bring family and you are a family member as far as I'm concerned. So would you like to come?"

"I'd be delighted. Thank you so much. Shall I meet you at the hotel?"

"That'd be good. We'll be leaving around nine," I said.

"I'll see you in the morning then."

We finished and I hung up. Penny was still snickering.

"Will you stop that?" I said. "I just don't want Buck to be alone."

"Yeah, right," she said and stood. She went to the bedroom and I was left alone with Willy. I looked at him and said, "Are you still on my side?" He yipped, put his head on my leg, and look up at me. He was so cute.

Penny came back out and said she was ready to go. She looked beautiful in her dress, a short black number with a low cut top showing her ample breasts. Probably boosted by a lift bra. She knew she had it and often flaunted them when it was needed.

Tonight, it was needed. She was also trying to impress classmates who knew her from school and from television. I was proud of her.

I stood, picked up Willy and handed him to Penny. I put on my jacket to cover my Glock and turned to her. "I'm ready."

"Try not to shoot anyone tonight," she said and led the way out of the room.

"I suppose you don't have your gun in your purse," I said, but she was already on her way to the elevators, ignoring me.

We went down to the car and drove to the banquet hall where the reunion was being held. I parked on the side and we went in. There was a banquet table decorated in the colors of our school, blue and gold. Behind the table sat Debby Sullivan, George Calley, Twyla Gawlas and Sara Swope. They were the types in school who led groups in getting organized. They were the cheerleaders for the class dances and events.

"Well, Jim Richards and Penny Wickens," George said. "Glad you could make it. Now the evening should be interesting. Are you going to solve a murder tonight?"

"Why? Is there going to be a murder and you have advance information about it? Should I look at you for the murder?" I said.

He squirmed a bit then said, "You're just well-known back here in town. I have no idea if there will be a murder."

Penny mumbled, "There better not be."

"May we sign in?" I asked.

"Oh, yeah, of course. I have to say, Miss Wickens, you are better looking in real life than on TV." He was turning red. I thought it was funny. "I'm sorry, I don't mean to be forward."

"Quite alright. I appreciate the thought. And it's Mrs. Wickens-Richards now." Penny leaned forward showing her ample breasts to him as she signed the guestbook.

He was trying not to stare, but glanced anyway. I had to laugh quietly. Penny was great at torturing men.

"Uh, Jim, if you'd sign in and find your badges," he stuttered.

"Oh, will you help put mine on?" she asked him, sounding like Marilyn Monroe.

I reached around her, signed in and grabbed my badge. Penny didn't have a badge since she wasn't a class alumnus, so I made up one for her from the blank badges. I wrote "Jim Richards' wife" on the badge and stuck it on her. She looked at it and grinned.

"Okay, I'll give you this." She smiled at George and we went into the hall.

Two women came up to me and ogled. I felt uncomfortable.

"Jim, it's so good to see you again. Wasn't it tragic about the cheerleaders?" said Pat Pollington.

"Pat, that was four years ago. Yes, it was tragic, but it's in the past now. We have to go on, don't we? Do you know my wife?" I said, motioning to Penny.

"Oh, my God. You're Penny Wickens! Are you married to Jim?" the other woman, Rebecca Besner, said.

Penny took the hand of the woman and said, "Yes, he lowered his standards to marry me. I had to compete with all his other women. He's such a stud."

I poked her in the ribs and said, "Now, dear, let's not exaggerate." I started to pull her away then turned back to the women. "Thanks so much, good to see you again. Where is the bar?"

Reunion Murders

Pat pointed to the back of the room and smiled.

I pulled Penny back to the bar and said, "You are not being funny. Well, actually you are. But be easy on the crazies."

"Yes, sweetie," she said and picked up a plastic glass from the bar. It was champagne and I knew it would go to her head.

"Easy on that stuff. Switch to beer later."

"I'll hold my liquor. I won't dance on a table," she replied.

"Or strip and fly around a pole? I hope not."

She looked around and said, "Do they have poles here?"

"No. So forget it." I turned and was looking at a man standing by, watching me. I didn't recognize him at first. When I did, I realized he was a classmate I didn't have much to do with in school. He was a decent person, but he was boring. He was a worse nerd than most and I knew he was rich now for the household inventions he created, ones that made it to television sales.

"Hello, Gary. How are you?" I asked, not really wanting an answer. But he answered.

"Jim Richards, I'm good. I see you stepped up in the world," he said, glancing at Penny.

"Yes, he did. I see you on the infomercials pushing your household toys," Penny said.

"Toys? My gadgets are big sellers. I have a mega-empire going on. You're a talk show host, aren't you?" He was being smug.

"Yes, I am, and I devoted one of my shows to your toys. More than half failed the tests put on by an independent testing lab. I liked the hamburger press though. It passed with flying colors."

"My gadgets are all tested thoroughly by independent labs to be sure they are reliable. You may have had a few bad products that you tested. I can assure you they all are reliable."

I knew my mother had bought a number of his crappy products, but I never argued with her. She found out for herself that they didn't work the way you see on the commercials.

"Well, Gary, it's good that you are doing so well. And that guy you have demonstrating your products on TV, he's a good pitchman," I said.

"Yes, Larry does a great job. He's a cousin and he has a talent for sales. You write books, don't you?"

"Yes, I do write books about my cases from my investigating firm in Las Vegas. They are best sellers."

"Sorry, I haven't read them. It must be interesting to solve crimes then to write about them. You must make good money," he said, smugly again.

"I do. Thanks and it was good seeing you. Take care. We have to mingle," I said, picking up another beer from the bar and pushing Penny away from the man.

"Don't shove. I'm glad to be away from him," Penny said.

"I was feeling like I wanted to buy one of his products and shove it down his throat. Something sharp." I looked over to the entrance and saw someone I wanted least of all to see.

It was Mark Jonsen.

*

Chapter 11

I felt a chill run through my body. I shook it off and watched him go to the registration table to sign in. He put on his badge and stood surveying the room. He didn't see me. I was too far away. He moved to the center of the room and stood looking around. He seemed to be looking for someone. I hoped it wasn't me.

Penny said, "What's wrong, sweetie? You look ill."

I carefully pointed out Jonsen and said, "That's my high school nemesis, Mark Jonsen."

Penny looked at the man and said, "He looks mean and dirty. Like he hasn't bathed in a long time."

"I'm not getting close enough to smell him," I said with a smile. I kissed her cheek. "Now you know my worst nightmare in high school."

"Why don't you go over and talk to him? See if he's changed."

I stared at her and said, "Are you crazy? I want nothing to do with the man. Now or ever."

I turned when I felt a tap on my shoulder. It was a friend from years ago. "Hey, Nash, how are you?" I said.

"I'm doing good, Jim. I hear you are doing well, too." He glanced at Penny.

"Yes, as you have noticed, I'm married to a celebrity. And a hot one at that." I laughed.

Penny smiled and said, "He doesn't know how lucky he is." She held out her hand, "As I'm sure you know, I'm Penny Wickens, and you are?"

"Nash Rawlings. Pleasure to meet you. I do watch your show. I enjoy your humor and how you question the guests."

"I like this man," Penny said to me.

I glanced back to see what Jonsen was up to. He was gone. I was going to enjoy myself and not worry about him. I turned back to Nash and said, "Would you like to take her from me? She's not easy to live with."

He laughed and said, "Thanks for the warning, but I'll let you keep her. I'm happily married now, to Cheryl Barton. Do you remember her?"

"Of course. She was one of the queen's court at our homecoming. Is she still good looking?"

"Well, she put on a few pounds, but she's still beautiful. Then again, I'm prejudiced," he said with a laugh.

"Nash, you always had a good looking girl on your arm. Cheryl is lucky to have you," I said. "So what are you doing now?"

"I'm an IT specialist at an Internet provider. I have to fix things when they screw up. Nothing worse than losing your internet connection. I get blamed for it."

"Can I call you when I have problems with my internet?" I asked.

"All the way out in Vegas? You pay for the ticket, I'll be there."

A rather chunky woman came up to us and latched onto Nash. I recognized her. It was Cheryl.

"Well, Jim Richards, how are you?" she said. "And I see you brought your wife, the famous talk show host. How are things in Las Vegas, the land of the rich and famous?" She sounded a bit sarcastic and rude.

"It's actually the land of the broke and unknown. The town does have its share of celebrities, but it's mostly hard working everyday people who come out to lose money or gain a little. It's not everything people make it out to be," I said, defending my new hometown. "We also have our share of crime and homeless people. So it's not exactly what you'd expect it to be, Cheryl."

She was quiet and then Nash said, "Well, we never got out there. It hasn't been on our vacation agenda."

"You guys should come out sometime. Penny and I will show you the real Vegas, not the glitzy glamorous city that you see in the brochures."

"I'd like that. If you'll excuse us, we have to circulate and visit." They went off, Nash pulling his wife away.

"She's an odd woman," Penny said to me.

"I think she isn't happy with her life. But we are, aren't we, babe?"

"Better believe it, my famous husband. Shall we circulate and visit?"

I laughed and we moved to another area of the room.

I saw a good number of classmates I recognized. Most had changed. The men had put on pounds and lost hair, the women gained a bigger girth and looked old. I was glad that Penny and I took care of ourselves. Well, I never exercise, but I get enough chasing down criminals. Or so I led myself to believe. Penny just had a natural beauty that didn't need much work.

I saw an old friend and told Penny to follow me.

"Hey, Paul, you still have all your hair, I see." One of my best friends, Paul, was a real lady's man and prided himself on his appearance. He was Italian and had dark black hair that was actually thinning a bit. I didn't want to bruise his ego by pointing it out.

"Jim, you old dog. I see you brought a date. Didn't the wife come with you?"

"Idiot, this is my wife, Penny Wickens."

"I knew that. Just yanking your chain. Pleasure to meet you, Penny. I'm Paul Primo, one of Jim's best friends from the old days."

"Pleasure to meet you, Paul. Funny, Jim never mentioned knowing you."

"Of course not. He didn't want you to know about me. I might have taken you away if I'd met you first," he said with an evil grin.

"Sorry, but I doubt that. I remember you from back in school. You were only two grades ahead of me, but you left a lot of girls crying in your wake. I prefer a stable man like Jim. Right, sweetie?"

"You got it, babe. So, Paul, what are you up to these days?"

"I own a couple pizzerias around the area. Paul's Pizza Parlors. We do a good business and have a good clientele."

"Are you still married to Mary?" I asked.

"Yep, thirty-nine years now, two beautiful daughters and four grandchildren."

"I never pictured you a married man. Especially all the times you were out with different women. I never figured you to settle."

"I just happened to find the right woman. She keeps me in line."

There was a loud shrill noise from the back of the room. There was a stage set up and a woman I recognized as Kathy Moore was at the microphone. "May I have everyone's attention? Please be seated as we would like to start the program we have for you tonight."

I turned to Paul and asked, "Is Mary with you tonight?"

"No, she had other plans and she didn't go to our school, so she opted out," he said.

"Too bad. Give her my best. Excuse us, we need to find our seats." Penny and I left Paul alone.

Penny leaned to me and said, "I remember him being such a womanizer."

"I'll tell you more personal stories about him later," I said, and we took seats at a table with three other couples I didn't recognize. Strange, I couldn't place their faces and the name badges didn't help. I was amazed that my mind had slipped that much.

Kathy announced that they had a few honors to give out. Some guy brought up an easel with a board on it. There were pictures attached to it. Kathy pulled one, looked at the back of the photo and said, "Is Martin Grolich here?"

That name shook me as it was the brother of Linda Grolich who was a cheerleader murdered back when we went through the cheerleader murders. I could feel Penny squeeze my hand. She'd been a friend of Linda on the cheerleader team. Martin and Linda were twins although not identical.

Reunion Murders

I looked around the room and saw him stand. Kathy called him up to the stage. He went up and stood next to her.

"Marty, you were selected back then as the class clown. I have a prize for you," she said. Someone handed her a bag. She opened it and pulled out a rubber clown mask. "After 45 years, this is your reward."

Everyone laughed. He stepped to the microphone and held up the mask. "This is going on my wall at home to remind me of all the fun I had in high school. But I want to say one thing. I see Jim Richards is in the audience and I never got to thank him for catching the killers of my sister. Thanks, Jim." He left the stage as everyone applauded.

I didn't expect that. I cringed and wanted to slide under the table.

*

Chapter 12

The ceremony went on for another hour. Everyone was given gag gifts for their most-likely-to role in the class of 1967. The most likely to succeed student was given a trophy for his being the classmate to not succeed. He was an insurance rep and lived an ordinary life with a wife and three kids.

Kathy spoke again. "We come to our last award for a person not on the most-likely-to list. The '67 alumni staff decided to add a special award. He was a simple, fun person in school, but ended up being pretty famous in his own chosen field. He has a movie about him, is a best-selling author about his exploits in crime fighting and owns his own private investigating firm in Las Vegas."

I suddenly realized she was talking about me. I cringed again.

"Let's bring up our most successful alumnus, Jim Richards." The people applauded loudly and Penny pushed me up. I didn't want to go. I hated the lime light. I didn't mind being known for my exploits but didn't like getting up in front of people wanting to honor me for it.

Reunion Murders

I reluctantly went to the stage and Kathy greeted me. She handed me a nice trophy and told me to say a few words.

I was just about ready to speak when there was a loud scream from out in the hallway. Everyone turned to the door as a waitress from the banquet hall came in screaming, "Someone's been murdered!!"

I could almost feel Penny's frustration that another murder happened near me. I dashed from the stage, gave Penny the trophy and ran to the door.

I got to her first as everyone else was stunned by what had just happened.

"Where's the body?" I asked the girl. She took me to another banquet hall across from ours. We entered and there above the stage was a woman hung up by ropes in a crucified position. Blood was flowing from her throat down her nice gown. I recognized the woman. It was Neena Martin. She was in my class and was very popular.

I went closer and pulled out my cell phone. I was going to call Trapper because I didn't have the local police on my speed dial. I could call 911, but Trapper knew everyone here and could get hold of someone who'd take care of this.

"Keep everyone out of here," I said to two young men, busboys, who came in from a side door. "Close that door and don't let anyone in," I said, pointing to the hallway entrance where people were starting to gather.

Trapper came on and said, "What now, Richards, another murder?" He laughed and then went quiet when I didn't respond. "Okay, talk to me."

"A murder. At my reunion. Can you get hold of someone locally to come?"

"I'm with Becker right now. It's his jurisdiction. Keep everyone away from the body."

"Thanks, it's not my first crime scene. Get Becker here quickly. He'll need crime scene people, too."

Trapper hung up and I turned to the girl still standing by the now closed doors of the hall. I could see people trying to look in the windows by the doors, all startled by what they saw.

I went to the girl and asked, "How did you find her?"

"I was supposed to check the room to see if it was set up for a banquet tomorrow, and when I turned on the lights, she…" The girl choked. "I saw her there."

"Okay, sit down over at that table and relax until the police get here." She went to the chair and sat.

I turned back to the body, looking up at her. Her blood was pooling on the stage floor. She couldn't have been dead for long. The ropes were strung over a light beam and tied off to a rack holding cables for the overhead lighting. It had to be a rather strong person to pull her up and tie it off.

One of the teachers from our school, Mr. Olsen, who was our class advisor, managed to get in and came to me.

"Jesus, is that Neena Martin?" he asked as he stood next to me.

"It is. Don't touch anything and get back from the stage. Forensics will be here shortly and they need the crime scene to be undisturbed.

"Yes, yes. I understand. Who'd do such a horrible thing?" he said as he moved back. I followed him to wait for Becker.

"Someone had it in for her," I said.

"Too bad it happened tonight for the reunion," Martin said quietly.

"Too bad it happens anytime," I replied.

"Yes, it is. I wasn't being callous."

"No problem. I understand. The police have been notified and we need to keep everyone out of here."

He went back to the closed doors and slipped out. I could imagine what he was going to say to the people. I waited for Becker.

About ten minutes later, Becker, followed by Trapper and three patrol officers, came in.

"You just can't escape your curse, can you?" Trapper said with a grin. "Who's the vic?"

Becker went to the body as I said, "Neena Martin. One of our group. I'd say she's been dead for about a half hour now." I pointed to the waitress and said, "This is the person who found her."

Becker went to the girl and sat on a chair next to her. He asked her to tell him what happened. She related the same story she told me. Becker came over to us.

"Crime scene unit should be here shortly. Will and I were at my place talking when you called, Jim."

I watched Becker as he talked. He seemed to be more mature than when I last saw him. He was growing into the role of detective, hardened by the crimes he had to solve. I liked the new Becker.

"What was going on when the vic was murdered?" he asked me.

"We were having a ceremony to give awards to students for their accomplishments," I said.

"Did they give you one for being the class snoop?" Trapper said with a laugh.

"No, for being the most successful alumnus. I was just about to give an acceptance speech when the waitress screamed."

"What did Penny have to say about the murder?" Trapper asked.

"Oh, crap. I forgot about Penny." I turned to the entrance and went out. I found Penny sitting at our table with three drinks in front of her. "I see you're taking this well."

She lifted one glass and drank from it. She looked up at me and said, "Why can't I take you anywhere without a murder?"

I sat next to her, lifted one of the beers and took a good swig. "Hey, I don't plan these things. They just happen."

"So what happened?"

I told her the details that I knew of and she just sighed, taking another drink. "Oh, well. It's your life and your destiny to solve murders. Who's taking the case?"

"Barry. I called Trapper to get hold of someone and he was with Barry. They are both here now."

"Good, you can let them handle this. Sorry you didn't get to give your speech for the trophy. It's quite nice actually," she said, lifting the thing and handing it to me. I studied it and put it back on the table.

"It's nice, but I didn't come over two thousand miles to get a trophy and a dead body. I'm afraid to retire and travel. There will be bodies left in our wake."

Penny laughed and kissed my cheek. "We can just stay home. I'll swim and you'll write your books."

"That sounds good to me." I looked back at the doors where the crowd was milling about.

"Go. Go investigate. It's what you are best at," she said.

"You have to come with me or I'll sit here and bug you."

She reluctantly stood and followed me out. People were all buzzing about the murder, spreading rumors already. The cop at the door stopped us and Becker yelled to him to let us in.

"Hey, Penny. Good to see you again, even under the circumstances," Becker said.

"It's good. I'm getting used to all this murder and mayhem around Jim. I should be used to it by now." She looked up at the body still hanging and shivered. "Well, maybe not too used to it."

Trapper said, "You should divorce him and find a nice quiet guy."

"Are you kidding? He keeps me in stitches with his exploits." She kissed me and smiled.

*

Chapter 13

The medical examiner helped to lower the body. The woman was tied in such a fashion that she looked to be crucified while hanging. Finally, they got her on the floor away from the blood pool.

Becker excused himself and went to the ME. Trapper stayed with Penny and me, watching the proceedings.

"How well did you know the vic?" Trapper asked me.

"Not very well. She was one of the snobs of the school. The queen of the prom and homecoming. Things like that. She ran with the money students, ones from well-off families. I was below her station in life so she never spoke to me. I really didn't care much for her. She was also a tormentor. You could call her a female bully and she lived up to it. I'm not really surprised by this."

"So it could be one of the victims of her hate?" Penny said. "I barely remember her. I never associated with the upperclassmen."

Reunion Murders

Becker came back and asked for my opinion on her murder.

"Well, I'm wondering something. I mentioned the incident that involved the student named Mark Jonsen. At one of the dances, Neena managed to get Mark out on the dance floor and two other male students pulled his pants down. He didn't have underwear on and he was enraged. Maybe he's worth looking into for this."

Becker asked, "Is he at this reunion?"

"As a matter of fact, he is. I saw him come in earlier. Shall we go look for him?" I said.

Penny said she was going back to the table to guard my trophy. I agreed and said to be careful.

"Don't worry, I'm armed," she said with a smile and went out.

"You have one dangerous wife," Becker said with a grin. "Shall we track down Jonsen? Since I already talked to him when we found his mother murdered, I know what he looks like. I may even look at him again for the mother's murder."

Becker, Trapper and I went out to the hallway and I asked a few people if they had seen Jonsen. Nobody seemed to know where he went. We checked the banquet room where most people went back to sitting, talking amongst themselves. Jonsen was nowhere to be seen.

Becker called to two of his men and asked me to give a description of Jonsen. I did.

"Search the building, everywhere, see if you can find the man," he said to the officers. They went off and we went back into the crime scene.

The shift supervisor for the Crime Scene Unit came over to Becker. "Barry, we got very little from the stage. The vic looks like she was strung up first and then cut. There were very few blood splatters anywhere else other than from around the hanging. I'll have more for you later."

"Thanks, Chet," Becker replied and looked at the stage. "This may have been premeditated."

"Revenge festering from years ago. If Jonsen planned this, maybe his mother caught on and he had to do her in," I said.

"Anything is possible at this point. I learned from you, Trapper, never to assume things."

"Good, grasshopper. You learn well," Trapper said with a grin.

One of the officers who were searching for Jonsen came in the room. "Becker, come with me."

103

Reunion Murders

We followed the officer as he went through a door at the end of the main hallway and up to a door marked employees only. We went through the door and found it was a restroom. The other cop was in the room and pointed to a row of stalls. Becker went to the last stall and found Jonsen, looking very dead.

"Well, this complicates matters," he said, looking back at us.

I went over and looked into the stall. It was definitely Jonsen. He was sitting on the toilet with a bloodied wound on his chest.

"Now we have a mystery," I said, moving out of the way so Trapper could see.

"Is that Jonsen?" he asked.

"In the flesh, on the toilet," I said.

"Okay, did he kill the woman and then himself? Or did he kill the woman then someone killed him?" Becker said to no one in particular.

"Yep, a real mystery," Trapper said to Becker. "Now what are you going to do?"

Becker turned to the cops standing by the door. "Go get CSU before they leave. Tell them they have to work overtime."

One of the cops left as Becker told us to get out of the restroom. We all went out into the hallway and stood waiting. Chet and his crew came into the hallway as Becker explained what we had found.

Chet smiled. "I needed the overtime." He went in the room followed by two of his team. We went back to the banquet room to regroup.

Everyone in the reunion was told to go into their hall and relax. Kathy asked if it was all right to serve dinner now.

Becker smiled. "I don't see any reason not to. You may as well make the best of this. We have the situation in hand, so go enjoy your reunion."

I moved to Kathy and took her arm, pulling her into the banquet hall. Everyone in the room turned to us as I waved to them.

I called loudly to the crowd. "It's okay, folks, the police have secured the scene, and it looks like they have found the killer." I told a small lie. "Now, let's go on and have a good time."

I saw the banquet food servers looking confused. "Hey, let's get some food in here," I said to them. They all scurried to do their jobs.

Kathy asked me what was happening.

"Nothing you need to worry about. Now, keep these people happy and eating their dinner. Get the band playing to relax everyone."

She went to the bandstand where the musicians were relaxing. They got up and Kathy said something to them. They started to play what I would call dinner music. I was glad they didn't play rock and roll. The group was stirred up enough.

I went to Penny and sat.

"So, what's going on?" she asked.

"Well, we suspected Mark Jonsen of murdering the woman. Unfortunately, we found Jonsen in a restroom stall dead. Big gaping wound in his chest."

"Oh, my," Penny said. "Did he kill himself or was he murdered?"

"Not sure yet."

"Should we be concerned for the other people in the room?"

I thought on that and kissed her. "You may be right. I need to talk to Becker." I stood and went out of the room.

Becker and Trapper were still by the back restroom watching the ME removing the body and complaining about having to come back.

"Can you check to make sure you have no more bodies before I leave?" he joked.

"I'll do a sweep and let you know. What are you complaining for? You're getting paid," Becker called as the ME went out. "He's a funny guy but I never know when he's being funny."

"Penny said something that could be pressing. Is it possible that others in the reunion could be in danger? There were two more men who did the deed to Jonsen. They could be in danger."

"Yeah, but with Jonsen dead, would they still be in danger?" Becker asked.

"It was a thought. Maybe post your men around the inside of the building to keep an eye out for the guests. It may relieve the tension."

"Okay, I can do that. We still have the crime scene open, so it would be justified to have them on guard." Becker called to one of his men and went to him. They talked and the officer took the mic for his radio and placed a call. Becker came back.

"He's calling for reinforcements to help. Who were the two men who panted Jonsen?"

Reunion Murders

"If I remember correctly, it was Ken Boggs and Donny Minter. They were friends of Neena and used to follow her around. They were like her bodyguards and did whatever she needed."

"Are they here tonight?" Becker asked.

"I'm not sure, I wasn't looking for them," I said.

"Let's go see if we can find them."

Becker, Trapper and I went back to the banquet hall and Becker went to the bandstand, interrupting the music. He talked to the leader and then took the microphone.

"Your attention, please. I need to know if there's a Ken Boggs and Donny Minter in the room."

The room went quiet, no one spoke. I was looking around the room and didn't see either man. I went to the guestbook and checked. Both of them had signed in. So where were they?

*

Chapter 14

Becker came down from the bandstand and over to me. "No one is coming forward," he said.

I pointed out the names in the book. "They were here, they're not now. That doesn't bode well for them. Now if they went out for a smoke or something, okay. But if they're dead somewhere in the building, you better find them quickly."

"Yeah. I don't want the ME to gripe at me again." He went out and over to the new men who showed up. "I want this place turned inside out and if you find anyone who doesn't work here wandering around, bring them to me." The men went off to search.

Becker turned to me. "You know, the cheerleaders were murdered. Now your alumni are going down. You come from a dangerous school."

"It wasn't much better back then either," I said with a laugh. "I'm going to find Penny and get some food. You two can work this out. I'm on vacation." I left Becker and Trapper, went into the hall again and over to Penny. She was already eating her dinner.

"Couldn't wait for me?"

"I had no idea when or if you were coming back. I was hungry. Ask and they'll bring you food," she said between bites.

I tracked down a server and asked for a dinner plate. She said she'd bring one over. I went back and sat next to Penny.

"So have you caught your killer yet?" she asked me.

"You give me too much credit, babe. Trapper and Becker are on the case. They'll find the killer in good time," I said as I felt someone come up behind me. I hoped it was my food but it wasn't.

"Hello, Ralph," I said when I turned to see the man standing there. "How are you doing?"

"Jim, I'm fine. Can you tell me what's going on?"

"You'll have to talk to the Detective in charge. I'm not at liberty to say."

"I hear it was Neena Martin who was killed. I didn't see the body, but I talked to people who did. I just want a few words about the incident to report to my readers."

"Readers?" I hadn't seen Ralph Franson since high school, and now he had readers? "What readers are those?"

"I write for a local newspaper, the Macomb Journal."

"Never heard of it. Is it new?" I asked.

"It is. It's a conservative paper and we investigate corruption in the local government, but we also do pieces of local interest," he said. "I think the murder of one of our outstanding alumni is something to report."

Crap. I assumed it was a scandal sheet for Republican viewpoints smearing Democratic opponents. I remembered Ralph being involved in political science classes and being head of the debating team. They had won a few competitions when they went up against other schools. Mostly they were a nasty bunch.

"Outstanding alumni?" I said. "Neena was a mean person. I'd hardly give her credit for advancing human relationships. Especially for what she did to Mark Jonsen. That was just cruel. Ken and Donny are as much to blame."

Reunion Murders

"Mark Jonsen was a bully. He terrorized our class without mercy. You should be just as glad that he got what he deserved back then."

"What did he deserve, Ralph?" I stood and faced him. I wasn't happy. "I didn't like Mark for the way he treated me, but he was tormented by people like you and Neena. As I remember, you were in with Neena's crowd. One of the high rollers. And you had no respect for people like Mark. You should be as much to blame for people like Mark. Now go away. I want to eat my food and you'll give me indigestion," I said as my food arrived. I took the plate and sat.

I started to eat and said quietly to Penny, "Is he gone?"

Penny chuckled and said, "Yep. You did him in and he skulked away."

"Good. I didn't like him in school, I like him even less now." I took a couple more bites of my dinner. "This isn't bad. What is it?"

"I haven't any idea, some mystery meat," she replied.

I was startled by Becker's appearance in the seat next to me. "To what do I owe the pleasure of this visit? I'm eating, as you can see."

"Sorry, Jim. I just wanted to ask you if you could come identify another body."

I turned my head to him and stared. "Another body? What is this? A convention of death?"

Penny was giggling and I looked at her. "You find that funny?" I said.

"Sorry, no. It's just your curse is going into overtime on this one," she replied.

I picked up my plate and fork and told Becker to lead me to the body. I followed him as everyone watched us go out. I seemed to be the center of attention tonight.

We went down the hallway again, out to a loading dock in the back. I was still trying to enjoy my meal.

"Sorry to bother you about this again," Becker said. "But you knew everyone in your class. Is this person one of them?" He pointed down to a body on the driveway leading up to the loading dock.

It was dark and I couldn't see the man on the ground very well. I went down the stairs on the side of the dock and over to the body lying in a pool of blood. I bent down and one of the officers turned his flashlight on the face of the victim. It was Ken Boggs.

"Well, this is disturbing. If Mark Jonsen wanted to kill the unholy three who panted him at the dance, he'd have to have done it from the hereafter." I looked up at Becker who had been joined by Trapper. "How long has he been here?"

"Haven't any idea. I called the coroner again. He was definitely not happy. He'll be back here shortly."

I was trying to wolf down my mystery meat and potatoes as I stood over Ken. I remembered him as being a friendly, jovial type. He fell in with Neena and her crowd and never got out. Too bad for him.

I went back up the stairs and followed Becker and Trapper back inside the building. I found a tub of dirty dishes and put my plate, now cleaned of food, in the tub.

"Okay," I said as we stopped in the kitchen. "Mark kills Neena for what she did to him at the dance, then he kills Ken, but who killed Mark? And why in the restroom?"

"We are still looking for Minter. He hasn't turned up dead so far," Becker said.

"Have you looked in any of the ovens?" I said, looking around the kitchen.

"That would be ghoulish," Trapper said.

Becker opened one of the ovens and it was empty. I think he was relieved. He pointed to one of his officers who were following us and they checked the other ovens, finding nothing.

"Okay, so no cooked Minter," I said, trying not to laugh at Becker's distress. He was sincere in trying to look good for Trapper. I figured he wanted to show he could do it.

"Have your men searched everywhere?" I asked.

"As many places as we could find. I had a couple employees go with my men to search places we wouldn't know about. They found nothing other than Boggs."

We could hear someone making noises coming down the hallway. It was the coroner.

"For crying out loud, Becker. Why couldn't you just ask me to hang around? I'll call all the wagons we have to stand by for more bodies. Or are you finished?"

"Hey, Harold, go easy on Barry. He's not responsible for all the bodies turning up around here," Trapper said to the man. "Just chill and wait until the area has been closed."

"I don't see CSU anywhere around. Are they privileged?" the coroner said.

"I called them back. They should be here soon," Becker said.

"Where's the new body?" the coroner asked.

"Steve, take him to the body," Becker said to one of the cops. They left.

"Now, can I go enjoy my reunion or do you think there may be another body?" I asked.

"If there is, I'll try not to disturb you," Becker said.

"Yeah, yeah, I've heard that already tonight," I said and went back out to find Penny.

*

Chapter 15

Penny was still at our table talking to some woman I didn't recognize. I sat next to my wife, listening to what they were saying. The woman was bubbling about Penny's show and all the guest stars she had on. Penny was telling her stories about some of the most embarrassing moments with a couple male guest stars. Ones I hadn't heard about.

"He actually kissed you?" I asked from behind Penny. She jumped when she realized I was there.

"I'll explain it later, sweetie," she said with her I-didn't-do-anything-wrong look. "Did you find the killer yet?" she said, changing the subject quickly.

I smiled. "No, we haven't. I'm hoping there are no more murders tonight."

The woman looked upset. "Murders? There were more than Neena?"

I looked over at her and said, "I'm sorry, but I don't know you. Did you graduate with my class?"

"Oh, no. I'm married to Brad Kennedy. We've been married since just after high school."

"Ah, yes, Brad." I wasn't fond of Brad back in high school and I doubted I'd be fond of him now. I don't expect people to change, especially the jocks in high school. They take on this persona that carries them through life. "I remember Brad. Is he still a jock?"

She hesitated. "He's changed since school. I went to St. Margret School for Girls, and we met at a carnival in Fraser. He picked me up, as they say, and we've been together ever since. It hasn't been a fairy tale life, but it's been good."

"I'm happy for you. How has Brad changed after all these years?"

She hesitated again. "Well, he's still fit, but he's gotten a little bigger."

"He was pretty tall, as I remember," I said.

"No, he's gotten wider. I love to cook and he loves to eat. He doesn't get as much exercise as he did in school on the team. Football was his love, next to me. He was supposed to get a scholarship to Michigan State, but he got turned down."

"Too bad. What's he do now, for a living I mean?"

"He works for K-Mart. As a manager. He's been there for fifteen years."

"I used to go to K-Mart a lot. I never saw him."

"He works up in the store in Sterling Heights. You probably went to the one in Fraser."

"I did. So where is good old Brad now?"

She looked around and tried to spot him. "He was over by the bar with a couple of his old team mates, but I don't see him now."

Old was the operative term. We all were old now and his team mates were probably not able to run the length of a football field. I sure wouldn't make it.

I turned to see Becker threading his way through the people milling about, heading straight for me. I cringed, wondering who had been murdered now. Three down, how many more? As long as it wasn't Penny or me.

He came up to us and stood looking worried. "Jim, could I talk to you out in the hall?"

Penny smiled. "Go ahead, sweetie. I'm having a good time talking to Doris."

"Doris? Oh, I'm sorry, I didn't get your name," I said to the woman. "Pleased to know you. Say hi to

Brad for me." I stood, kissed Penny, excused myself and followed Becker out of the room.

We were out in the hallway and I saw Trapper was talking to a couple uniforms. He turned when we came up. "Jim, we got our man."

"Oh, really, who?"

Becker said, "Donny Minter. A patrol cruiser saw him weaving on Groesbeck Highway and pulled him over. They say he was drunk. They've got him at the station and forensics is checking him over. He's pretty much out of it, and he's not saying much."

"So. no more dead bodies?"

"Nope, they're all done. The coroner has gone off with the new ones and CSU didn't find much. The officers who pulled Minter over found a knife in his car. Blood work will tell if it's the weapon."

"Jonsen had a possible knife wound in his chest. There should be his blood on the knife." I said.

"We'll know better tomorrow. When is the alumni picnic?" Becker asked.

"It starts around ten, if the weather holds. Feel like coming? You too, Trapper. My treat."

"Since you're treating, I'll go," Trapper said. "I like bar-b-ques."

I looked at Becker. "Now you'll have to come, just to keep an eye on Trapper."

"Depends on this case. I'll see," Becker said as an officer came up and whispered something to him. "Okay," he said and turned back to us. "I have to go talk to Minter, I'll see you two tomorrow." He went off with the officer.

Trapper grinned. "Our little boy has grown up, hasn't he?"

"He's your little boy. I never claimed him. Although I like Barry, and he is maturing into a good detective. We'll see how he handles this case. Now, I haven't been devoting a lot of time to my wife or the reunion. So do you want to come in and relax with us?"

"At a class reunion for old folks? No, thanks. I'm going to watch Becker beat on Minter."

"Keep me informed. I can't believe Donny would do all these murders. He wasn't a bad person. He just followed Boggs and Neena in their bad deeds. See you tomorrow."

"I'll meet you at the hotel and follow you to the picnic," Trapper said and went off.

Reunion Murders

I went back into the room. Now Penny had a small crowd around her. It always amazed me, no matter where we were, she'd draw a crowd. I guess that was expected when she was seen by so many people from her show. I made my way through the people and sat in a chair one seat away from her. I didn't want to move any of her admirers.

She was talking about Vegas and her adventures. I loved listening to her talk. She was looking at the people around her and then saw me. She smiled and paused.

"I'm sorry, but I need to talk to my husband, the great P.I., and find out what's going on."

Everyone laughed and left us. I moved over next to her. "So what's going on?" she asked.

"They think they caught the killer."

"Who?"

"Donny Minter. I don't think he did it, but time and forensics will tell. I'm sorry I haven't spent much time with you."

She smiled. "I'm used to it by now. I happen to be an independent woman, and I love you dearly, but I can get along without you."

Bob Moats

That had me worried. "I hope you don't get along too much without me."

"Never. I know you love chasing crime. Now shall we dance?" she said as the band started to play.

People were heading out to the dance floor. It was almost comical, watching all the seniors trying to do the electric boogaloo or whatever the band was playing. I lasted on the dance floor until I was ready to give out. We sat.

A few more of my classmates came up and talked about the old times and what we were up to now. Around eleven, I told Penny I was wearing down. We slipped out quietly.

Willy was resting quietly in the car. He jumped up and barked as I opened the door.

"Good guard dog. Do you need to run?" I clipped on his leash, took him to the grass next to the hall and let him do his thing. I figured that no one would be walking there, so I left his gift.We drove back to the hotel and went up to the room. I was surprised to see Buck resting in the hallway. "What are you doing here?" I said as he got up off the floor.

"My brothers were getting drunk and I didn't feel like sticking around. I enjoy being sober. I didn't know when you two were coming back and didn't know where you were, so I came here."

"How long have you been here?" I asked.

He looked at his watch and smiled. "About a half hour. No problem. So how was the reunion?"

"Have I got things to tell you," I said as I opened the door.

*

Chapter 16

"So you had a good time at the reunion?" Buck asked as he sat in an easy chair.

"Three murders. And they think they caught the killer, but I have my doubts. I could be wrong, though."

"Wow, three murders. You need to ramp back on your curse, man," Buck said with a loud laugh.

"I don't have a curse," I replied.

"Yes, you do," Penny called from the bedroom.

"You stay out of this. Go to sleep."

She came out wearing her silk pajamas and a fluffy robe. She plopped down next to me on the couch.

"I was there, remember. I know your curse is real."

"Fine, now let's talk about my former classmates behind their backs," I said with a laugh.

We talked for about an hour, Buck filling us in on his adventures with his brothers. He also said he had plans for tomorrow and he wouldn't be able to make it to the picnic, then Buck said he was tired and left.

I called Trapper to see what Becker found.

"So what's going on?" I asked when he answered.

"By the time I got to the precinct, Becker was trying to wake Minter. He had passed out from being drunk, so Barry couldn't talk to him tonight. He's going to give Minter the night to sober up and then hit him in the morning. How was the rest of the reunion?"

"Well, I've had tooth extractions that were more fun. It was nice to see a few people I did like. If it wasn't for all the excitement over the murders, it would have been boring. Where are you now?"

"I'm with Barry. We're in a bar in Mt. Clemens."

"Any place I know?"

"Nope, it's new. We moved away before it opened. It's in an old bank building and the thing is crazy the way it was designed."

"I knew that place when it was a bank. Then it closed down and became a dance club a few times, but never made it. So it's open again?"

"Yep, now it's a DJ bar, lots of flashing lights and lots of young girls."

"Well, don't get too involved with the women. You're not a young stud anymore. Besides you can't take one home to your mom's house."

"We have Barry's apartment to crash in. I think I may end up there anyway. I already told Mom I would be there for the night. But I'll see you for the picnic. Barry may be tied up so he may not come."

"Okay, see you then." I said my good-bye, he didn't, and I hung up.

"So what's happening on the interrogation?" Penny asked.

"Nothing. The suspect passed out from drinking too much and they're letting him sleep it off. Trapper said he'd still like to go with us in the morning."

"That should be fun. I'm going to bed," she said and stood. "Are you coming?"

"In a minute. We're three hours ahead of Vegas, so I think I'll call Lynn and Deacon and see how they're doing on their murder."

"Say hi for me, and tell them we're ahead by two murders," she said with a grin and went to the bedroom followed by Willy.

I hit the speed dial for Lynn and waited. She answered after four rings. I could hear a baby crying in the background.

"Should I ask how things are going?" I said.

"Not if you want an honest answer. I need a sound proof room for the baby. What's up?"

"Just calling to see how your murder case is going."

"Peachy keen. We're interrogating suspects and getting nowhere. Feel like coming back?"

"I've got my own murders to investigate. Or I should say, Trapper has to investigate with his old partner Barry Becker."

"You have murders?"

"Three of them. I beat you. They think they have the killer, but I don't know. I may stay over one more day to help find out who murdered my old classmates."

"Where did this all happen?"

"Right at the reunion, while we were celebrating. They were killed in the banquet hall in different areas."

"Nice. Penny has to be back for her show on Tuesday, doesn't she?"

"Yes, I may send her back on the jet with Buck to return to their jobs. I can come back out on a commercial flight, whenever. Trapper can stay or go, it's up to him. Then again, this may all be for nothing, the suspect may confess in the morning and we'll all come back together. I'm only going to stay because these were classmates of mine."

"Say hello to Deacon. I just put you on speaker."

"Hey, Deacon. I was just telling Lynn about my three murders out here," I said.

"So what's the details?" Deacon asked.

I went over the night in detail and then finished.

"Well, that's different," Deacon said. "Almost like your vengeance killing of the cheerleaders after all these years. You have some classmates who are time bombs."

I laughed. "Doesn't every school have the nut jobs?"

"Mine did," Lynn said. "A couple of them are in prison for various crimes."

"Speaking of crimes, do you have any suspects in your murder?" I asked.

"We are looking at a couple. One was romantically involved with the vic, the other has a background in theft of money from his previous jobs in casinos. Never convicted, flimsy evidence. I'm now thinking my man wasn't skimming money. I talked to Vito and he is giving us free rein to investigate his people."

"Hope it goes well. I'm going to get some sleep now. I have a picnic to go to tomorrow."

"Your reunion has a picnic too?" Lynn asked.

Reunion Murders

"Actually it's an alumni picnic for all the school years. They have it every year and it brings in young and old alumni for a twenty-five year span. It just so happened to be the day after our reunion this year. I don't mind the picnic. There are a number of underclass grads I'd like to see again."

"Just don't let Penny catch you." Lynn laughed. "Old girlfriends can be dangerous, too."

"My only girlfriend was murdered during the cheerleader murders. But I'll be careful. Thanks and I'll call tomorrow night." I hung up and stood. It was quiet in the bedroom when I went in. Penny was asleep but snoring softly.

I undressed and slid into the sheets that we brought with us. Not that I didn't trust the cleanliness of the hotel, but I've seen too many forensic investigations where the sheets in motels were full of body fluids.

Willy was resting next to me and sighed. I held onto him until I fell asleep shortly after.

The next morning the sun was streaming into our room again. I got up and dressed. Penny was in the bathroom getting ready for the picnic. She came out and had on short shorts and a tank top. She wasn't hiding her attributes. I laughed.

"What's so funny?" she asked.

"Nothing, really. You're just so good looking, the men will all be tripping over their own feet."

"Thank you, sweetie. I like hearing that. Are you ready?"

"We have to wait for Trapper," I said just as there was a knock at the door. "Talk about timing. I like that man."

I went to the door and opened it. It was Trapper and he was alone.

"Becker couldn't make it?"

"He's wanting to interrogate Minter. Feel like watching?"

"Can we?" I asked quietly, not wanting Penny to hear.

"Sure we can," Penny said from behind me, causing me to jump.

"Will you stop creeping up on me?" I said.

"Now you know how Lacey feels. Can we go to the interrogation?" She asked Trapper.

"Becker called me and said he was going to question Minter by 8:30, so there will still be time to get to the picnic."

Penny slapped me on the back and said, "Get moving, we have a suspect to beat."

We all piled into the SUV I rented and I drove up to the Clinton Township precinct. The banquet hall was in Clinton Township so it was Becker's jurisdiction. We went into the building and up to the front desk.

"Crap, Trapper, what are you doing back here? Not looking for your old job are you?" the desk officer said.

"Hell no, Karl, I love it in Vegas and my job. Sun, warmth and babes. How are you enjoying the winters here?"

The big cop laughed and said, "You here for Becker?"

"Yep, I need to evaluate his performance. To see if he's worthy of the badge."

"Too bad someone didn't evaluate you," the cop said with a hearty laugh.

*

Chapter 17

We left the laughing cop and went into the homicide squad room. Trapper knew his way around the building very well since he spent almost fifteen years there. We found Becker at a desk in the squad room looking over some papers.

"What, they can't give you a private office?" Trapper said to Becker as we came up.

"Things are tight here. I'm lucky to have a desk. You here to see me question Minter?"

"I wouldn't be in this place if it weren't for that. How's he doing?" Trapper asked.

"He woke slowly but he's in room 3 still sobering. I wonder if he drank so much at the reunion that he was as bad as he looked."

"I didn't see him," I said. "But he could have gotten soused if he drank quickly. The bar was open."

"Well, he's in rough shape. I have the feeling he'll say he doesn't remember last night. He's all we have and forensic says the blood on the knife came from Jonsen. So we have him for that."

"Did the prints on the knife match his?" I asked.

"There were minimum prints, but they were his. We just need to find out what happened to the woman and man. I'm ready to talk if you want to watch."

"Lead on," Trapper said.

We went down a hallway passing officers who were greeting Trapper. He was still popular. We came to a door marked interrogation 3. Becker pointed to the observation room and he went in. We went into the room and sat looking through the magic mirror.

"How's your head this morning, Donny?" Becker asked, looking down at the man.

Minter looked up through blood-shot eyes and uttered a sound that sounded like a wounded dog.

"I hope you'll talk more than a grunt. Now, can you speak?"

"I don't know why I'm here. I didn't do anything."

"Well, other than drunk driving, we also have you for murder. Now that's something."

Minter raised his head and stared at Becker. "Murder? What murder? I don't remember any murder."

I could imagine that Becker wasn't happy right now, hearing the drunken amnesia excuse.

"Your friends, Neena Martin and Ken Boggs. Oh, and we can't forget Mark Jonsen. We have the knife from your car that killed Jonsen. Now do you remember the murders?" Becker asked.

Minter just sat staring. Then he said, "Neena and Ken are dead? I didn't know, really."

"Okay, Donny, let's assume you didn't know they were dead. We figured that Jonsen wanted them dead, but maybe you killed Jonsen. Did he try and kill you too?"

Minter was leaning on the table holding his head in his hands and moaning.

"I didn't know," he said again. "Did Jonsen really kill them?"

"We don't know. But we're sure he didn't kill himself. The knife we found with you is his murder weapon. I just need your story, Donny. Maybe you were protecting yourself from Jonsen and fought with him. Is that what happened?"

Reunion Murders

"I don't know!" Minter cried out. "I can't remember."

Trapper turned to me and said, "He may have traumatic amnesia. Jonsen came at him, they struggled, and Minter killed him."

"I don't see Donny for murder, so I'll buy your theory. Could be self-defense," I said.

"I'd say it was. But we'll leave that up to Becker."

Becker sat down across from Minter and leaned forward. "Okay, Donny, you don't remember. Is there anything you do remember from the reunion? Do you remember going to it?"

Minter was quiet for a moment, thinking. He sat back, closed his eyes and didn't move. "I remember Ken and me arriving at the hall at the same time. We planned that. I remember signing in at the reception table and going to the bar. I don't remember drinking that much, but I must have. Could I have killed Jonsen?"

"The knife has your prints and the blood on it is from Jonsen. I'd say we have evidence enough that you did it."

"I don't remember," he said quietly.

"Why did you leave the reunion so early?"

"I don't remember."

"What happened to Jonsen?"

"I don't remember."

Becker slammed his hand down on the table, shaking Minter into an upright position.

"You better start remembering something. You are going down for the murder of Mark Jonsen and maybe I'll throw in the murder of Neena and Ken."

Minter started sobbing and dropped his head to the table. Becker sat back watching the man then looked to the mirror. He stood and left the room, coming into observation.

"Let him stew for a bit. He'll come around," Trapper said.

"I hate to say it, but I think there's something more to this. I need to call the lab and see how much he had to drink." Becker pulled his cell phone and pushed a couple buttons.

"Ernie, Barry Becker here. Did you get results on Don Minter?" He listened for a bit then said, "Thanks," and hung up. He was quiet for a moment then said, "They say he couldn't have been drunk,

137

blood alcohol was too low, but they did find drugs in his system. Ones that could have made him look drunk. They don't have all the results on what he was on yet. They'll let me know. Either he was taking something or he was given something."

"The plot thickens," I said.

Becker turned to me. "Can't get much thicker. I'm figuring Jonsen murdered Neena and Ken in retaliation for what they did to him in high school. Then he caught Minter in the john and tried to kill him. Minter fought and stabbed Jonsen."

"What about the drugs in his system?" Trapper said.

"I'll have to explore that further. He could be a drug addict. We'll know better when we find out what he was on," Becker said.

"So, not much more to go on. It's pretty cut and dried," I said to Becker. I looked at Penny sitting quietly next to me. "Shall we go to the picnic?"

"About time. This was boring," she said. "I was waiting for the rubber hoses to come out."

"Penny, my dear, they stopped using rubber hoses long ago," I said.

She stood. "They should bring it back. Let's go."

I looked at Becker. "Since you don't have much to do now, feel like going with us? Maybe you can interrogate the other alumni."

He thought on that and said, "Not a bad idea. You can point out a few people who may have had it in for Minter."

"Do you think Minter is being set up?" Trapper asked.

"It's something to explore," Becker said. "Why not? He was drugged and turned loose with a murder weapon. Why would he keep the knife? I'm going to have him taken back to his cell to calm down." He stood and went out.

I stood and followed Penny out of the room. Trapper came out shortly after. Becker was talking to a uniformed officer and the cop went to take Minter to his cell. Becker came back to us.

"I'm ready to go."

"You and Trapper can follow us or go together and follow. Whatever, just follow." I led Penny and Willy out of the station and got into the car. Trapper and Becker went to Trapper's mom's car and followed. Becker knew where the park was that we were heading for but they stayed behind me.

Reunion Murders

About twenty minutes later, we pulled onto Stevens Park and up to the area where they had a snow fence and a tent set up to contain the people. I wasn't fond of seeing snow fence in the summer but it was functional. We got out and waited for Trapper and Becker to join us.

At the entrance to the picnic, I was greeted by a number of old classmates. Old was the word. They looked like they aged badly. But they were in a couple grades ahead of me so I wasn't too upset.

"Jim Richards! You made it," came a voice I did recognize. I turned to see a woman who was one of the officials in the alumni association.

"Hello, Jane. Yes, I flew over two thousand miles just to be here," I said. "As I'm sure you know, this is my wife Penny. Penny, this is Jane."

"Pleased to meet you. Are you a friend of Jim's?" Penny asked.

She just laughed and said, "Hell, no, I hated your husband."

*

Chapter 18

"Well, I loved you too, Jane," I said.

"Oh, Jim, I never hated you as in hate. You were just a pain in the ass when you were doing the alumni website. So you just didn't win favor from me," she said.

"I wanted it done right. The guy who took it from me made a mess out of it. Or that's my opinion. Now can we sign in to enjoy the festivities?"

She laughed and pushed the paper to us to sign. "These two gentlemen, and I use the term loosely, are friends of mine. I invited them," I said.

"They look like cops. Are you bringing them here to investigate the murders from last night?"

I smiled. "Yes, the tall young one is a cop and the old one is one of the investigators from my firm."

"Hey," Trapper said. "I'm not old."

I looked back and said, "You're older than Becker, so you're old." I finished signing Penny and me in then took Penny into the area. Trapper and Becker signed in and followed us.

We stood looking around for anyone we knew and possibly wanted to see. This picnic covered twenty-five years of classes up to 1990. I wanted to see the classmates who were around my time, but mostly from Penny's year of 1969.

Becker asked, "Anyone here I should talk to?"

"Sure," I said and took him to a table of people from my class. "Hey, everyone, survive what happened last night?"

There were seven people at the table and they all eyed Becker. They probably remembered him from last night.

Amy Tapia spoke first. "It wasn't pleasant. Ruined my night and I'll dream about poor Neena hanging from the ceiling for a long time to come."

Becker moved forward. "I don't want to accuse anyone, just ask a few questions. It's better than asking all of you to come in to the precinct to talk in interrogation. Now, can I have a moment of your time?"

They all looked at each other and agreed. Becker sat at the table and introduced himself. "I'm detective Barry Becker from the Clinton Township police. The banquet hall where the victims were murdered was in my jurisdiction so I'm investigating."

"Victims? There were more than Neena?" asked Sandy Sillman.

"Yes, Ken Boggs and Mark Jonsen were also victims."

"Oh my god, we weren't told," said Karen Meinburg-Richwine.

"Why were they killed?" asked Roland Hansen.

"We don't know at the moment, we're still investigating, which is why I'm asking questions now. So let's start with you," he said to Sandy. "Where were you in the reunion when Neena was murdered?"

"Hey, I was with a bunch of people who will back me up. I was never alone all night."

Becker smiled. "I believe you." He turned to the others and asked, "I presume all of you can vouch as to where you were last night?"

They all voiced their whereabouts for the night before at the same time. Becker raised his hand and asked for quiet. "I have Don Minter in custody. We found him last night with a knife that had Jonsen's blood on it. Do any of you know where Minter was during the reunion?"

Karen spoke first. "I saw him going out into the hall alone just before we gave out the awards. I seem to remember seeing Ken going out after him. Did Don murder Ken too?"

"We think that Jonsen did that. Did anyone see where Jonsen was at any time?"

Roland said, "I was watching him because he was fascinating. He was so strange looking. I never cared for him in school. He was a bully. I thought he looked pathetic now. I was wondering how his life brought him to look the way he did."

"Explain, please?" Becker asked.

"He just looked pathetic, dirty and had a crazy look to him. I'm a psychologist, and I watch people to study them."

"You use the term crazy?" Becker smiled.

Roland laughed. "I may be a shrink, and I hate that term also, but he just looked crazy. You think he may have killed Neena and Ken?"

"As I said, we are investigating," Becker replied.

I was watching the people and noticed one person was being quiet. "Shirley, did you see anything last night?" I asked.

She jumped and looked up at me. "I didn't see anything. Really. I was busy talking to friends."

"And you are?" Becker asked Shirley.

"Shirley Davies. I was a friend of Neena's. I was sad to hear what happened to her. But I didn't see anything. Sorry."

"No problem. Did Neena give a hard time to anyone else other that Mark Jonsen?" Becker asked.

Everyone at the table looked around to each other, not saying anything. Finally Roland said, "Neena terrorized a lot of people, even me. I wouldn't kill her for it, but the thought had been there. She was merciless in her pursuit to be the meanest she could be. I'm surprised someone waited this long to do her in."

"Did Boggs or Minter do any bullying, or did they just follow Neena?"

"Followed," Karen said. "Kenny and Don were nice guys but Neena really wrapped their heads around her finger. They followed her like little puppies. If you have Don in custody, I'd look elsewhere for Neena's murderer."

"Would you say Jonsen could have done it?"

"He could have," Amy said. "He was not well in the head after they embarrassed him in front of his classmates. I was a friend of Kenny's, and he didn't approve of what Neena was doing. I told him he should distance himself from her. I hate to say it, but I think Neena was having sex with both of them."

Trapper leaned to me and said quietly, "Yes, the great leveler, sex." Penny heard him and made a tsking noise with her tongue. He looked back at her and smiled. She rolled her eyes, moved away and walked to a small group of women talking near us.

I had to laugh to myself even though Becker was doing well. I was surprised that Trapper didn't butt in on Becker.

"What about Jonsen? Anyone know what he was like? Recently, I mean," Becker asked.

"I only saw him a couple times in the last year," Shirley said. "He was usually taking his mother around to the store or the post office. That's all I know about him."

Roland said, "I live in Chicago now, so I never saw him after graduation."

Sandy said, "Mark lived down the street from me. I saw him a number of times going to and from his mother's house. He lived with her."

"Did you know his mother was murdered?" Becker asked.

Everyone expressed surprise and then Sandy said, "I wondered why all the stuff was out on the curb the other day for trash pickup. It looked like Mark was cleaning house. I guess he was throwing all of his mother's stuff out."

"Probably," Becker said. "We're still investigating her murder. Jonsen is going back on my list of suspects."

"You think he may have murdered his mother?" Amy asked.

"We probably won't know now that Jonsen is dead. But I think he may have done it. If any of you have something that you remember, contact me at the Clinton Township Police precinct."

Becker stood and thanked everyone. He led Trapper and me away from the table and out to the middle of the yard. I looked over and Penny was talking to three women in a group.

"So. what do you think?" Trapper asked Becker.

"Honestly? I have no idea. You have a clue?"

"I think Donny is still the best suspect you have. Prints, blood and motive," Trapper said.

"Self-defense?" I asked. "Good motive for murder."

"You think Minter murdered everyone and is claiming innocence?" Becker said.

"Could be. Do you think you can bust him down and get him to confess?"

"Only if I can use the rubber hose." Becker laughed.

"Excuse me, but I have to go see what lies my wife is telling all her former classmates. I need to protect my reputation," I said.

"Or what's left of it," Trapper said with a laugh.

*

Chapter 19

I walked over to Penny and came up behind her. She was talking about her show and Vegas. I didn't hear any damaging mentions about me, so I came up and tickled her ear. She jumped and turned to hit me.

I covered and laughed. "So, bragging about your accomplishments?"

One of the women said, "We are so jealous of Penny. Are you Jim?"

"I am and I deny everything she told you about me."

"Even the nice things?" Penny asked.

"Okay, I'll give you that," I said. "Now, you know me, who might you be?" I asked the women.

Penny introduced us. "Jim, this is Karen Grams, Gail Chesney and Shirley Alvarez. They were in my classes back in…well, a few years back."

"By almost half a century," I said.

Reunion Murders

She hit my arm. "Why don't you go chase a murderer or something so I can gossip with my friends?"

"Fine. Nice to meet you girls." I walked away and ran into a man I knew nearly a half a century ago.

"Hey, Jim, how you doing?" the man asked.

I sort of liked the guy, but he was not someone I wanted to hang around with. Nick Glidden was his name and I was going to be nice.

"Nick, how are you?" I asked politely. I was beginning to wonder why I even came out here from my safe home in Vegas.

"I'm fine. I hear you're a detective now."

"Private Investigator. There's a small difference. I work for myself, detectives work for the police. What are you into now?"

"I'm a cop," he said with a smile. "To be exact, a detective. Out in Port Huron. I'm attached to the St. Clair County Sheriffs."

"I used to live in Port Huron years ago. My son was born there. They do have enough crime to keep you busy."

"They do, and it's getting worse. Drugs and unemployment have pushed the crime up. Everyone needs a quick fix."

"Well, I'm glad you're on our side, Nick. You still with Peggy Janley?"

"Nah, we broke up years ago. I never married her and it was good I didn't. I married a great girl from Wadhams. She worked in the shopping plaza on Lapeer and Wadhams Road."

"I remember that place. I always said there were nothing but beautiful women around that area."

"And my wife was one. I hear you married a celebrity," he said and I nodded. "I followed your situation back when the classmates were being murdered. Even had one of your detective friends come out to look for one of the cheerleaders up in Lake Port."

"That was Will Trapper and he's here now with his old partner, Barry Becker."

"I'd like to meet them. Just to talk about old times," he said with a smile.

I looked around and saw Trapper and Becker standing by the grills, looking hungry.

Reunion Murders

"Follow me," I said.

I took Nick over to Trapper and introduced them. I explained about the past connection and told Nick I would talk later then left them to reminisce. I went back to Penny who was talking to a bigger crowd now. All admirers I presumed.

Penny smiled at me when I came up. "Sweetie, come and meet my fan club."

I went to stand next to her and grinned. "I'm not a celebrity like my wife, so just ignore me."

The people laughed and then I saw Becker coming our way. He excused himself through the people and whispered in my ear, "Can I talk to you?"

I excused myself and followed him. We went off to the side of the area where Trapper and Nick were standing.

"Jim, Nick was telling us something interesting. Did you know that Mark Jonsen had a brother?" Becker said.

I thought back and vaguely remembered that fact. "His brother was older, as I remember. Not in my class like Mark. What about him."

Nick said, "His name is Steve Jonsen and he's bad news. He lives in Port Huron and has been in and out of jail a number of times. He always called his brother, Mark, to bail him out each time. Mark would come up and get him out. The last time Mark bailed Steve out was two weeks ago. I heard them talking and they were mentioning the reunion. I heard Steve ask if the woman would be there. Mark said he was sure she would be. I don't know what woman they were talking about, but you have a dead woman now and suspect Mark. Get the connection?"

"Do you know where Steve is?" I asked.

"I know where he lives if you want to talk to him."

Becker got a grin on his face. "We sure do. Maybe he's a key in this."

"I hope so and I hope you put him away for a long time. I'm tired of seeing his ugly face."

Becker took out his notebook and wrote down the address Nick had in his phone for recent cases.

"This may help since Mark is dead and so is his mother. Steve is now an orphan and has no one to bail him out," Becker said.

"Good, get him out of my jurisdiction."

Reunion Murders

"We hope to, thanks," Trapper said. "Let's get some refreshments and some of this good looking food."

"I'll talk later," I said. "I need to go rescue Penny from her fans."

I left them and found Penny's crowd had grown. I was surprised she wasn't giving out autographs. When I got to her, she pulled me down to a chair next to her and whispered in my ear, "This is fun."

"I hope you enjoy it. Don't forget, we still have to go visit my family after we're done here."

"I haven't forgotten. Let's just enjoy our day here."

"You mean that you want to enjoy your day here. I'm just surviving."

"That too. These are all my classmates and I'm the only one who made something of myself out of my class." She kissed my cheek. "Just like you did, sweetie, from your class."

"We'll have to go through this again next year for your reunion," I said.

"Good. It will be nice to get my trophy. We can put yours and mine on the mantel."

"We don't have a mantel. I'll have to install one."

Penny turned back to her fans and they asked more questions, ranging from hunky male guests to her favorite star. She was loving it. I just sat and watched.

About a half hour later, Penny excused us from her friends and we went to get some food. Trapper, Becker and Nick were sitting on a picnic table eating and talking. Penny and I got our food and joined them.

I introduced Nick to Penny and he gushed over meeting her. "Nick, she's just a woman. Maybe a famous woman but nevertheless just a woman, and my wife."

Penny laughed and shook Nick's hand. "Never mind Jim. He's just jealous that I'm more famous than he is."

We ate our food and had good conversation. Penny forbade us from talking about the murders so we talked about the fun we had in school.

Around five, I said to Penny that we should leave. She agreed. We had visited with all the people we wanted to see and avoided those we didn't want to see. It actually was more pleasant than the reunion, and the weather held out.

Reunion Murders

We got back to the car and Penny put Willy in the back. We took him with us but he slept through most of it. I hoped he was alright.

We drove to my mom's house and got out. Penny turned Willy loose, and he made a bee line to my mother, bouncing around her feet.

My brother and his family were there, as were my son and his family. We sat and talked for a while, having a nice visit. Later, my brother caught me coming out of the bathroom and took me to the living room.

We sat and he said, "So, what's going on with the murders from last night?" My brother graduated five years after I did from the same school, so he knew most of the people from our school.

I explained the events of the night and he sat listening. "So, you don't have any witnesses to the crime?"

"Nope, everyone was enjoying the reunion. We do have one small lead now. Just have to track down Jonsen's brother and see what he knows."

"Jonsen had a younger sister, too. She was in my class."

That surprised me. "I didn't know that. Do you know where she might be?"

"Last I heard she was dead."

*

Chapter 20

"Dead? How'd that happen?" I asked.

"Not sure of the exact details. I heard she was killed in a fight at a bar in Detroit. Hit on the head with a bottle that caused her death. I don't know who hit her, just that she died," my brother said.

"Interesting. That family sure likes to die violently. We're going to try and find the last living member of the family to question him on Neena Martin's murder and what he may know."

"I thought you were flying back tomorrow."

"I'm sending Penny back with Buck. I'm going to stay until we solve this or I get tired of Michigan. Either way, I'll be here a little longer. I'm not telling Mom or my son, so keep that to yourself."

Reunion Murders

He said he would and we went back outside where the others were. Around nine, Penny and I said our good-byes and left. We went back to the hotel and up to our room.

"So, you're still going to stay over?" Penny asked.

"Just for a couple days. Don't go having any wild parties while I'm away."

"I may sell the house and move so you can't find me."

"I'll just move into your dressing room at the studio," I said with a grin.

"So you found out Mark had a big brother?"

"Yeah, I almost forgot about him. Nick said he and Mark were plotting something for the reunion. He wasn't sure what, they didn't say, but it may have been premeditated murder on Mark's part with his brother's help. We're going up to Port Huron tomorrow to find Steve Jonsen."

"After you take me to the airport."

"Yes, and I better call Buck to see if he's ready to go."

I pulled my cell phone out and sat on the couch. I called Buck and waited.

"Hey, Jim. What's shaking?" he said when he answered the phone.

"Just checking to see if you're ready to go back tomorrow?"

"I am. When will you two be ready?"

"Penny is going back, I'm staying a day or two more to help find out what happened to my classmates."

"You aren't going back?" he asked.

"No and neither is Trapper. You can go back to be sure things are running smoothly in the office."

"Hell, the office can run itself. Lacey keeps everyone in line and Earl and Lynn are there."

"True. Are you saying you want to stay too?" I asked.

"If you don't mind."

"Well, I don't mind, but you'd have to go back by commercial airlines. I'm not going to rent another jet."

"Oh, that means I'd have to go through all the crap they do to search for bombs and weapons?"

"Yep, the TSA and their x-ray machines."

"I'd rather walk. Besides, Penny will need me to drive her back home in the limo. You have fun. I'll see you in the morning to go back to Vegas."

We finished and I hung up. Penny came out in her pajamas and robe and plopped down next to me. Willy sat at my feet until I picked him up and set him next to Penny.

"So, is Buck ready to go?" she asked.

"Yep, he'll meet us in the morning."

"Good, because I don't want to have to drive the limo home."

"No, he said he'll do it."

"Good. How long do you think you'll be out here? We've never been apart for very long, other than when I've been kidnapped." She smiled and poked my ribs.

"You'll love being alone without me. You can run around the house naked and I won't be there to attack you."

She mulled on that for a moment. "True, I never thought about it in those terms. Okay, you enjoy your stay here and I'll run naked." She stood, taking Willy with her to the bedroom. "Don't stay up too late. I may start practicing being naked." She winked and went into the room.

It didn't take me long to figure out what she meant.

Early the next morning we had our bags packed. At least Penny's bags. I went down to the front desk and made arrangements to stay on for a couple days longer. Buck called saying his brother was dropping him off. Trapper called to confirm that I was staying. I said I'd go to the precinct and meet him and Becker there. Buck arrived and I drove him and Penny to the airport.

"Don't go getting in trouble out here. I can't get back to save you," Buck said as we loaded the bags on the jet.

"I'm sure Trapper and Becker will save me. You just guard Penny and take care of the office. Tell Lacey what's going on and see if Lynn needs any help with her case. I'll be fine."

"Will do, brother. You be good and stay out of strip clubs."

Penny gave me a sideways glance and said, "I'd better not hear about you going into strip clubs without me."

I went over and gave her a kiss. "Never. You'll never hear that I did."

She gave me a puzzled look. "That's not what I meant. Just don't do it."

"Yes, dear."

The pilot said they had to go. I waved as Penny, Willy and Buck got on. The jet closed up and the pilot must have been given clearance to go.

I stood watching the jet take off and had an empty feeling. My two best friends were leaving me behind.

Now to solve the murder so I could get out of there myself. I went back to my rented car and reminded myself to call the car place to extend my rental. I drove up to the Clinton Township precinct and parked. As I was going to the entrance I heard my name being called. It was Trapper coming from his mother's car.

"So did Penny and Buck get off safely?" he asked.

"Yep, they're on their way. I'm feeling a little lost without Penny around."

"Enjoy yourself. You two act like you're joined at the hip. Everyone needs a little time to themselves."

"I guess so. Shall we go solve this so we can go home?"

"You just can't get away, can you?" he said with a laugh.

"Nope," I said and we went into the building.

Becker was at his desk on the phone. He waved to us and we went over and sat. He finished his call and said, "That was Nick up in Port Huron. He's going with us to make it official. He's not wanting to see Jonsen again but if it will get him out of his town, he's all for it."

"It's about an hour ride up there. We can take my SUV, it's more comfortable," I said.

"Well, if we have to take Jonsen in custody, we'll need a police unit," Becker said. "So thanks for the offer, but we have to be official about this."

"We could put him in the trunk," I offered.

"Nope, won't work. Sorry." Becker stood and we followed him to the motor pool to get a car. They had a plain Crown Vic with screen mesh separating the front from the back to transport prisoners.

I looked at Trapper. "You can ride in the back. I'm riding shotgun."

Reunion Murders

He grinned and got in. We drove out and over to I-94 freeway heading to Port Huron. I had driven the route many times in the past and it was pleasant but long. We chattered about the case, giving our theories, but didn't come up with any answers.

The trip went smoothly and we exited off the freeway and went over to Lapeer Road then drove into the town to the police station. Becker called Nick just as we got into town and he said he'd wait for us outside the jail entrance.

We came to what was the courthouse and jail combo. Nice. Go from court to jail without leaving the building. Nick was standing outside talking to a uniformed officer.

"Hey, guys, this is Ken Oland," Nick said. "He's going with us to Jonsen's in case he gets out of hand. Jonsen is not a nice customer. Ready to roll?"

We went back to our car as Nick and officer Oland went to the police cruiser. We followed them out and over to 10th Street going south to what was called the red zone. It was mostly very old housing that transient people rented to live in before they got evicted for not paying rent.

We drove down a side street and pulled up to a house badly in need of repair. Everyone exited their cars and went up to the porch.

"I'll handle this until I say you can question him," Nick said. He banged on the door and we waited.

After a few minutes a woman answered.

"What the hell do you want now, Glidden? Steve isn't here."

"Do you know where he is, Barbara?" Nick asked.

"Probably getting drunk at his favorite bar. Now go away." She slammed the door.

"Well, that was rude," Trapper said.

*

Chapter 21

"That was Jonsen's girlfriend. She's put up with Jonsen for a while now," Nick said. "She can't bail him out, she lives off Jonsen. He does have a part-time job as a cart shagger and stocker at the Kroger on 24th street. The money he makes he spends mostly on drinking at the Active Lounge. He's probably there now."

Reunion Murders

Nick headed back to the car as we followed. The cruiser drove up 10th street to the corner of Lapeer where we pulled into the parking lot. The Active Lounge was a bar that I knew well. I'd been there a few times. Okay, too many times. We entered the front entrance after Nick told Oland to go wait by the back exit in case Jonsen ran out.

It was dark and the band hadn't started yet, it was too early. Nick knew Jonsen and went straight for him. The bartender saw us coming and leaned across the bar to Jonsen to say something. Jonsen stood and started for the back door. Nick ran after him and we kept up.

Jonsen hit the back door and ran into Oland. The cop was a solid 280 at least and built like a linebacker. Jonsen went down hard when Oland clocked him.

We came out and picked up Jonsen. I could see a little family resemblance in him to Mark. He yelled, "Whatever it is, I didn't do it."

Nick was shaking him and said, "Steve, we just want to talk to you. Now settle down. I should take you in for running. But I'll be nice and we can talk out here."

Jonsen straightened his clothes after Nick released him. We had him surrounded and he couldn't get past us now.

"What the hell, you brought an army with you?"

"Nick, shut up and listen. You know you and I went to the same school." Nick looked at me and continued. "This man and I were in the same class as your brother Mark."

Jonsen looked at me and said, "Yeah, so what?"

I said, "Your brother was murdered last night." I could have been gentler about it, but he wasn't someone I would be gentle with.

He didn't react. He just stood there not saying anything.

"You knew he was murdered, didn't you? At his reunion," I said.

He was thinking over his options, I figured. He could lie or make up a story. "I didn't know that. How'd it happen?"

"You don't know? It seems you and your brother were talking about the reunion at your old high school and plotting something. I heard you when Mark came to bail you out the last time," Nick said.

"I don't know what you're talking about. We didn't plot anything."

"Maybe I should ask Barbara where you were last night. Unless you have an alibi. Got anyone I can call right now to say where you were?" Nick pressed him, getting close in his face.

Jonsen looked around, the sign of a man trapped and trying to find a way out. "I was home all night, watching TV with Barbie."

Nick pulled his cell phone and stepped back. He dialed a number and waited. "Hey, Barb, it's your favorite cop, Glidden. I'm talking to Stevie and I was wondering just what time did Steve get home last night? He says around midnight."

Jonsen looked panicky and Oland grabbed onto his jacket and held him in place.

"Oh, really? That's interesting, I thank you for that. Talk again some time." Nick hung up and grinned widely. "Yeah, I'll talk to her again, at your trial for murder." He moved back to Jonsen.

"Your alibi tells me you were gone all night," Nick said. "You told her this morning when you got back that you stayed at your mother's house all night. That's not too far from the reunion, is it? Now shall we go to the station and have a nice talk?"

Jonsen was silent as Oland pulled him to the cruiser and put him in back. Nick turned to us and said, "Shall we go beat him into a confession?"

Becker, Trapper and I went to the Crown Vic and followed Nick back to the station. I had never been in this precinct when I lived here. I was a good boy back then. Oland took Jonsen to an interrogation room and stood guard outside.

Nick invited Becker in since it was his original case and told Trapper and me to go to observation. We went in and settled in the chairs to watch Jonsen sweating now.

Nick and Becker hadn't gone in yet. I could see them talking outside the room, probably plotting an attack. They were laughing, then went in, still laughing. Jonsen was startled when the door flew open.

Becker sat as Nick walked around the room, occasionally leaning into Jonsen and staring.

"What the hell are you doing?" Jonsen yelled.

"I'm trying to figure how I want to have you prosecuted. Why don't you explain why you were at your mother's house last night? And you must know your mother was murdered. Did you do that too?"

Reunion Murders

"NO! I didn't. Mark did that. The idiot, he just couldn't keep his cool. He had to get mad and killed her. I can't forgive him for that, but I understood. She was a mean, crazy woman."

"So what was this plot to murder the woman at the reunion?" Becker asked.

"Murder? No, we didn't murder her. Mark told me he wanted to embarrass the woman by grabbing her and stripping her naked, tying her up and then pushing her into the reunion. We got there and she was already dead, hanging from the ceiling. Mark said he was going to be sick and went to a restroom in the back. I waited around a hallway for him. He didn't come out so I went to the back and into the restroom. I found him dead on the john. I got out as fast I could. I knew I would be blamed for both murders."

Becker looked at Nick and then back at Jonsen. "You didn't see anyone around the area where your brother was murdered?"

"No, man. If I had, I'd have beaten the shit out of him for what he did to my brother."

I was beginning to wonder about Minter now. Maybe he did the murders. He caught Mark Jonsen in the john and did him in after he murdered Neena and then Ken. This was getting complicated.

"So you're saying you didn't do anything at the reunion?" Becker asked.

"No, man. We had a plan but it didn't include murder."

"Did your brother have other ideas?" Nick asked.

"What? That he wanted to kill the woman? Hell no! Mark wanted to embarrass the woman, not kill her."

"What about Ken Boggs? Did Mark want him dead too?"

"Boggs? No, Mark said he knew Boggs was a puppet for Neena. He didn't want to get back at him. He didn't want anyone murdered. Will you stop saying that!" Jonsen was getting agitated now and Nick backed off a bit.

"Okay, Steve, start over from the beginning," Nick said.

Jonsen paused and sat back in the chair. He exhaled and said, "Mark came to me and said he wanted revenge on the people who embarrassed him in school. Mostly Neena. He knew they would all be at the reunion, so we planned to go there and grab the woman and embarrass her. He didn't care about Boggs and Minter. He just wanted Martin. I drove up to the house and picked him up, then we went to the

171

reunion. I waited in the car while Mark went in to see where Martin was. He called me and said he couldn't find her. I went in and we went into the other hall because I didn't want to be seen there. That's when we looked in the back of the room and saw the woman hanging."

Becker's cell phone buzzed and he excused himself from the room. It was Ernie from forensics. "Hey, Ernie, what's up?"

"They got the tox on Minter. He was definitely given a slow-acting hallucinogenic drug. Why he was given that, I don't know. He also had no blood on his clothes from either vic, so he couldn't have stabbed Jonsen or Martin unless he changed clothes after he murdered them. There was no blood from Boggs either. So I'd say Minter probably isn't the killer."

"Well, that's interesting. Anything new from Minter?"

"You'll need to talk to him. He's starting to come around from the drug. He says his memory is clearing up."

*

Chapter 22

Becker went back into the room and whispered something into Nick's ear. They quietly conversed for a moment then Nick stood.

"Steve, relax, we may let you get off with minor charges. So just be good," Nick said to the man looking worse for the occasion. Jonsen nodded.

They came out of interrogation as Trapper and I came out of our room. "What's happening, guys?" I asked.

Becker told us what forensics said. I had the feeling Minter was innocent.

"So, I think we know enough from Jonsen to say that he was a victim of his brother's vendetta. Minter is starting to come around with his memory, and we still don't have a suspect." Becker didn't look happy. "We need to go back and see what new story Minter has."

"I can hold Jonsen for leaving the scene of a crime and being stupid. Do you want to take him or shall I keep him? Please say you'll take him," Nick said with a grin.

"Sorry, you can keep him. I have enough on my plate with three murders," Becker said.

"Let me know what you find out. I knew Boggs and Minter from school. I also knew that Neena Martin was a bad influence on both of them. I hope Donny is innocent."

"I'll let you know," Becker said and turned to Trapper and me. "Shall we take a ride back?"

We said our good-byes to Nick and went out to the car. The drive back was just as long and we talked about the Jonsen family and their troubles.

We arrived back at the precinct and went over to Becker's desk. He had called ahead and had Minter put in a room for questioning. "We'll let him stew for a bit then go talk," Becker said.

Becker's desk phone rang and he picked it up. "Becker, homicide," he said. He listened for a moment then thanked the caller. He hung up and said, "That was the ME. He said Neena Martin had sexual intercourse just before she was murdered."

"Was she raped?" I asked.

"He said it looked consensual, it didn't look forced, and her panties were on backwards. Looked like someone dressed her after she was murdered. Oh, and she had the same drug in her system as Minter had."

"This gets stranger and stranger. Someone has sex with Martin, kills her, redresses her and hangs her up for the world to see. I don't see Mark Jonsen going to all that trouble," I said.

"Maybe Jonsen spiked Martin's drink and Minter's. Jonsen got her into the other hall and had his way with her while she was under the effects of the drug," Trapper said.

"No good," I said. "Remember, Jonsen had his brother with him and they found her already dead."

"You just love tearing up my theories, don't you?"

"Every chance I get. Now we need to see what Minter is remembering and solve this."

Becker stood. "You two can sit here and deduce all you want. I'll go talk to Donny boy."

We followed Becker to the interrogation room and Trapper and I went into observation. Becker went in the room where Minter sat, looking much better than the last time we saw him.

Reunion Murders

"Don, you look all refreshed. How are you doing today?"

"I now remember what happened that night. I want to get it on the record. I didn't murder anyone," Minter said.

"We already have an idea that you didn't, but what do you know of the murders?"

Minter leaned forward on the table. He put his hands flat and smiled. "It started with Ken and me sitting at a table when Neena came over. She sat next to us and said she was horny. I used to have occasional sex with her back in school. She never cared much for Ken, so he never got any. She was talking to me about going to another room and doing it. The thrill of doing it on our reunion night, she said. Ken didn't say anything, but I could tell he wasn't happy. Neena took a vial out of her purse and said it was something to stimulate the sex. She put it in my drink and hers and we drank."

He paused and asked for water. Becker waved to the cop outside the door and told him to get a bottle of water. He went off.

Minter continued, "Neena said she'd be in the room across the hall and I should follow her. I waited, then left to go over. We did it on the stage then I must have blacked out. I was groggy, but I remember I was being taken to my car."

"Who took you to your car?"

"I'm pretty sure I know who it was. I was having trouble focusing, but I'd swear it was Brad Kennedy. He was a big jock in school, and he was hot for Neena. That's all I remember. I passed out in the car and when I came to, I just drove away to go home. I have no idea how the knife got in the car." Minter sat back and went silent.

Becker waited but Minter just sat there looking lost. "Okay, Don, wait here. I'll be back."

Becker left the room and came around to us. "Jim, do you know this Brad Kennedy?" he asked.

"I do. As a matter of fact I talked to his wife the other night at the reunion. She didn't know where her husband was. He had gone off somewhere. If Brad was hot for Neena in school, I wonder if he wanted to renew old feelings for her. He may have found Minter doing the deed to Neena, got mad and did her in."

"But why put Minter in his car?"

"Okay, we need to establish a timeline for this." I said. "Minter and Martin are doing it when Kennedy comes in and finds them. Don was already passing out from the drug Neena gave him. Kennedy murders Neena, by stringing her up and slashes her neck.

Reunion Murders

Maybe Ken came in and saw this and ran with Kennedy following with a knife. Ken gets murdered, then Kennedy goes back to the hall and hears the Jonsen brothers coming. He hides in the restroom where, shortly after, Mark Jonsen comes in and finds Kennedy. They fight, Jonsen is killed and Kennedy leaves just before Steve Jonsen comes in, finds his brother and runs. Kennedy takes the knife and Don out to his car and dumps him and the knife in, figuring Don would be blamed."

Trapper and Becker just stared at me. Trapper looked at Becker and said, "You know he's going to put this in his next book."

"It's just a theory," I said.

"Well, I like it," Becker said. "But now we have to find Brad Kennedy and question him."

"His wife said he works at the Sterling Heights Kmart. The only one I know out there is at 18 Mile and Dequindre Road," I said.

"I know a couple cops in Sterling. I can have them meet us," Trapper said.

"Well, call them and let's go." Becker told the cop at the interrogation room door to take Minter back to his cell.

Trapper stopped his call and said, "How do we know he'll be there?"

I pulled my cell phone, did a web search on Kmart and found the one we wanted. I tapped the phone number of the store and my phone connected me. I just love these new smartphones.

After a couple of seconds, some woman answered. "Sterling Heights Kmart. How may I direct your call?"

"Yes, is Brad Kennedy working now? I need to talk to him."

"Yes, Mr. Kennedy is in, hold for a moment," she said and put me on hold. I just hung up.

"Okay, he's in. Make your call," I said to Trapper.

Ten minutes later we were on the road to Kmart.

*

Chapter 23

We pulled into the parking lot and met with Trapper's cop friends on the side of the building.

"Trapper, just couldn't stay away from us, could you?" One cop held his hand out to Trapper.

"If I knew they'd send you, I would have protested. How are you, Enright?"

"I've been better. What's the deal here?"

"We have a suspect in three murders over in Clinton Township. He's a manager here."

"The reunion murders? I heard about that. You aren't on the force anymore. Why are you here?"

"This is my former partner, Barry Becker, sergeant over in Clinton Township. The old man is Jim Richards, P.I. from Vegas." Trapper smiled at me. I would have given him the finger but it wasn't the right time. "Jim and I work in the same firm. Jim came out here for the reunion and called Becker when he found the dead vics. I tagged along to visit family."

"So you think the killer works here?" he said to Becker.

"We have it on good authority he does. We need to question him, but the evidence so far says he had a big hand in the deaths."

"Well, lead the way," Enright said and we went to the front of the building and inside.

Becker went to the front customer counter and asked for Brad Kennedy. The girl at the counter picked up her phone and made a call. We stood waiting, two uniforms and us. We were quite a sight.

I watched down the main aisle to the back where there was a door to the stock room. The doors opened and out came a person I hadn't seen in years. I also hadn't seen him at the reunion. I guess he was busy killing people.

He came down the aisle and was about twenty feet from us when he stopped and looked like he was evaluating the situation. Becker moved forward and asked if he was Brad Kennedy. Brad suddenly turned and ran back down the aisle.

We ran after him and through the doors into the back room. We didn't know the layout of the room but Brad did. The uniforms split in two different directions as Trapper, Becker and I moved through the middle of the room. It was filled with pallets of products and many tall shelves of goods. He could hide in there for a long time.

Becker yelled, "Kennedy, we just wanted to talk, that's all. Now you've gone and looked suspicious. We have Don Minter for the murders at the reunion but need to talk to you as a witness." He lied.

There was no sound as we walked around. Then we heard doors open and turned to see Kennedy run out of the room and back into the store. Trapper yelled to his friends and we all went back out.

I listened for his footfalls and could hear someone running. I headed that way followed by Trapper while Becker went with the police straight to the front doors. I looked up at the signs over the departments and saw he was heading to Sporting Goods. I had a feeling I knew what he was up to. Guns.

I stopped and told Trapper. We pulled our weapons and went carefully to the area. I heard cabinets being opened and knew they only had rifles, no hand guns. I told Trapper.

"Rifles, hand guns, they both still shoot," Trapper said.

"Go that way around the aisles. Try not to shoot a customer," I said.

"Take your own advice," he said and went down the side aisle to the main aisle. I went down the back aisle along the back wall. I suddenly saw Kennedy pop out from a side aisle and aim a rifle at me. I ducked quickly in the aisle next to me as I heard the shot fired. I went low to the ground and brought my head out to see Kennedy was gone. I heard two more shots fired and then it was quiet.

Becker spoke over the store PA and asked all customers to go to the front of the store and evacuate immediately. I ran down the side aisle, carefully looked down the main aisle and saw Trapper. I signaled to him and went around the next aisle. Kennedy was still not in sight.

I could see down another main aisle to the front of the store and saw people streaming out. Enright was at the door watching for Kennedy to slip out. I turned to see Kennedy coming up behind me on the aisle with his rifle aimed at me. Just as he fired, I dropped down and barely missed being hit. Trapper came around the back and took a shot at Kennedy. The man screamed and went down on the ground. I came up and over to him, grabbing the rifle from his hands. Trapper came running up and smiled.

"All in a day's work at Kmart," he said.

Kennedy was rolling on the floor, having been hit in the hip.

183

I bent down to him. "Did you think you'd get away?"

"Screw you, Richards," was all he said.

Becker came running up with Enright. "He's yours if you want him," Enright said. "He's part of your investigation."

Becker pulled his cell phone and placed a call for an EMS unit.

We carried Kennedy to the front door and waited. The EMS showed up and put Kennedy in, strapping him down on the gurney. Enright had to report the incident and two detectives showed up. Luckily they knew Trapper and it was like old home day as they talked.

After everything was back to normal for the store, we left.

"Now we'll have to question Kennedy in the hospital. I'd prefer we could do it in the station," Becker said.

"I don't know why he assumed we were after him for the murders," I said.

"He was feeling guilty. When he saw cops, he panicked. Just shows he did it."

"Well, we still need the story if he'll come across and tell us," Becker said.

We arrived at the hospital where they took Kennedy. Becker had called for a couple officers to watch Kennedy while he was being patched up. Two hours later he was ready to travel. The doctors said it wasn't serious, just that Kennedy would walk with a limp for a while.

Becker had him taken to the precinct and put into a cell next to Minter. "That should shake him up." Becker laughed.

Becker had to go report to his captain about the incident in Sterling Heights. Trapper and I sat at his desk until he came back.

"The captain is happy that we cleared this up," Becker said when he returned. "They wheeled Kennedy into interrogation. It was easier to put him in a wheelchair than to carry him."

"I doubt he's going to admit to multiple murders," I said.

"Barry will drag it out of him," Trapper said with a smile.

A uniformed officer came to Becker and said, "Becker, Minter wants to talk to you."

"Thanks, Dave," he replied. He stood and we followed him to the holding area. Minter was in his cell and jumped up when he saw us come in.

"Jim, I'm remembering more now. When they put Kennedy in the cell next to me, it brought back more memories. I was on the floor of the stage just after I passed out, but I came to long enough to see Kennedy pulling up Neena with ropes. I pretended to be out and watched him. I was weak and couldn't do anything, then I must have passed out again. It's all coming back now."

Becker went to the cell and asked, "You'd be willing to testify as to what you saw?"

"Neena and Ken were my friends. I'd hang the bastard myself if you'd let me."

"Good, I'll need you to give your statement to one of our officers. Be patient and we'll have you out of here shortly." Becker turned back to us and had a big grin on his face. "I think this will clinch it."

*

Chapter 24

We went back to the squad room, and Becker sent a detective to take Minter's statement. "Shall we go let Kennedy in on the good news?"

We went to interrogation and Becker let us come into the room with him. Kennedy was handcuffed to the wheelchair and he wasn't looking happy.

"I ought to sue all of you for my discomfort," he spit out angrily.

"You're going to be more uncomfortable where you are going, Brad. We have a witness who saw you murder Neena Martin and is willing to tell it to the jury. I'm sure you'll have plenty of time to get comfortable in prison."

Kennedy went silent, staring at us.

"Now, you want to tell your side of the story?" Becker asked.

Kennedy didn't say anything for a couple minutes. We waited.

Reunion Murders

"What the hell. Yeah, I killed the bitch. I came in and found her and Minter rolling on the floor. Minter had passed out and Neena was trying to wake him. I pulled Minter off her and said I could finish the job. She just laughed and asked how a fat man was going to pleasure her. She laughed at me and called me fat. I hated her for that." He went silent again.

"So you murdered her," Becker said. "Did Boggs catch you doing it?"

Kennedy looked up and sighed. "Yeah, but I dealt with him. I pulled my buck knife and stabbed him. Took a couple good stabs to get through his bulk. Then that idiot Jonsen almost caught me. He said I killed Neena. I had to stop him too."

"Didn't you get blood on yourself?" I asked.

"The banquet hall had a locker room for the staff and I found some clothes to fit. I put the ones I had in a hamper. Then I took Minter out to his car, planted the knife and let him take the blame."

"Too many holes in your plan, Brad. It did you in," I said.

Everything that was said in the room was being recorded and would help to put Kennedy away for a long time. We left the room and Kennedy was taken back to his cell. Minter was in the squad room sitting at a desk with a detective taking his statement. He smiled at me as I passed by him.

"Well, it's over and I want to get back to my life in Vegas. I've had enough of Michigan," I said.

"Thanks, guys," Becker said to us.

"Feel like coming to my hotel for a little beer and chips?" I said.

"How about a pizza to go with that?" Trapper said.

"Fine with me," I said and we left Becker to finish up the paperwork for the case. He was going to join us later.

I was in my hotel room relaxing while Trapper watched TV. We waited for Becker to show before ordering the pizza. I called Buck to see how everything was going and told him about the case and finding the killer. We finished and I called Lynn, putting her on speaker so Trapper could hear.

"Hey, employee, how's your case going?" I asked when she answered.

"We solved it without you," she said with a laugh. "It was a rival embezzler who didn't like the competition. I'm liking my new role as a P.I. and not having to put up with the police hierarchy. Deacon is going to take the lieutenant's test later this week. I'm pulling for him. How's your case?"

"It really wasn't my case. It was my friend Becker, Trapper's old partner. We caught the guy and he'll be seeing the inside of a prison for a long time."

"So you'll be coming back soon?"

"Tomorrow. I called for reservations for Trapper and me. We fly out of here at nine and arrive around ten your time. A three hour flight in one hour, not bad."

"Have you talked to Penny yet?"

"I'm calling her after we finish. I don't want to interrupt her wild party," I said with a laugh.

"What wild party?" came a familiar voice. It was Penny.

"What are you doing on Lynn's phone?" I asked.

"We're on speaker, and you called Lynn before you called me. You're in big trouble, mister," she said. That was the woman I loved.

"I have no excuse. Now, do you want to know who the killer was?"

"Yes, tell me, was it Minter?" Penny sounded excited.

"Nope, Brad Kennedy."

"Who?"

"Remember, we talked to his wife, Doris, and she didn't know where he was. He was out murdering people. That Brad Kennedy."

"Oh yeah, the jock. I never trusted the jocks when I was a cheerleader. Is he dead? Did you shoot him?"

I had to laugh. "No, dear, Trapper shot him in the hip. He'll live to spend his life in prison. Are you and Lynn having fun?"

"I'm at their house with the baby. She doesn't cry when I hold her."

"I never cry when you hold me," I said.

"That's too much information. Now go have fun with Trapper and Becker but no strippers!"

Lynn said she'd talk to me more about her case when I got back and we hung up. Trapper looked at me and said, "Women, don't ya love them?"

Becker showed up and brought pizza with him. We sat eating and relaxing then around eleven the two of them left and I crawled into bed, thinking about Penny.

The next morning Becker dropped off Trapper. Trapper said his so-longs to his friend as I did too, and we went to the airport. I called to have the car picked up, then we endured the searches and having to explain our guns. They reluctantly let us on the flight but our guns were being held until we arrived in Vegas. I hated commercial flights but luckily it was a good trip.

Buck came to pick us up and drove us to the office. Penny was there with everyone else. It was a nice homecoming. I asked Lacey how the addition was doing. She stood and took me to a new door on the side of the lobby and we went through it. I was shocked that the addition was finished and the women had gotten it all set up. The offices for Lynn and Buck were real nice and the lounge was great.

"How did you get all the furniture in here so quickly?" I asked.

Penny smiled and said, "I know all the right people."

I gave her a kiss and said, "You did good, babe. I even like the foosball table."

"Want to try and beat me?" she said.

"I'll beat your pants off." I turned to the others and said, "Everybody out, Penny is going to get naked."

THE END

For every ending there's a new beginning.

~~*~~

Here's a preview of the next book "Big Apple Murders"

Chapter 1

"So, what do you do for a living?" the woman asked as she removed her dress and sat on the edge of the bed to remove her nylons.

"Don't start an interview with me. You're a hooker, so hook. I'm paying you for a couple hours in bed — the works. That doesn't mean talking." The man stripped down to his boxer shorts and excused himself to go into the bathroom.

The woman dropped the rest of her undergarments, and naked, crawled under the covers of the king size bed. Her john had picked one of the nicer hotels in New York City. They even went up to the room together as husband and wife. He said she wasn't dressed like a tart, which is why the man had chosen her. They didn't draw suspicion.

Bob Moats

She was relaxing, waiting for him to come out of the bathroom. The door finally opened. He stood in the doorway silhouetted by the light behind him. The main room was dark save for one small lamp in the far corner. It wasn't enough to fully illuminate the man.

He slowly walked towards the bed, the glow of the lamp revealing what he wore – a mask. A Halloween mask of a skeleton face covered his whole head. The woman thought of the Grim Reaper, only the man had no hooded robe on. He was naked.

"Hey, I didn't sign up for a kinky trip, mister. What's with the mask?" she said, as he crawled over to her on the bed.

"You are going to make love with the devil tonight, bitch," he spoke from behind the mask.

She started to move out of the bed, but he grabbed her and pulled a noose he had previously attached to the bed post around her neck. He tightened it so the woman couldn't move away. She wanted to scream but he tightened it more, cutting off any sound she could have made.

"I want to look into your eyes as the life goes out of you," he said as he hovered over her and waited for her to strangle to death.

Reunion Murders

~~*~~

Penny was not happy with her hair that morning. She was trying to get ready to leave for her job as host of her talk show in Las Vegas, which was broadcast through a network to the country.

"This won't do!" she yelled as she tried to get a brush through her hair. I was standing just outside her bathroom door wondering what her problem was. "Damn hair," she said as she fought with the brush.

"Babe, your make-up and hair girls will fix it. Besides, you look cute with your Albert Einstein hair-do," I said, and had to duck when the hair brush came flying out of her bathroom.

"I hate bed-head!" she yelled, as I retreated from the bedroom with Willy, our toy Yorkie, following at my heels. Even he knew it was good to get out of her way.

I went to the kitchen to make my toast, and I even fixed Penny's oatmeal. She came flying out and said not to bother with her breakfast. She was going in early to have her groupies fix her rat's nest. She always referred to her make-up girls as her groupies because they were always around for her. She gave

196

me a quick kiss, lifted Willy into his travel purse, and was out the door in record time.

I hoped she didn't rush to work in her car. The chances of a ticket or an accident worried me. But I knew she was careful, she valued her life.

I sat munching on my toast and watching the local news. I hated to watch the news, but this morning I felt like it. I don't know why. I finished the toast and the news and got dressed to go into the office. The office was nicer now, with the addition built onto the side of my building for Lynn and Buck to have their own work space. Plus, there was a lounge for us to relax away from the perils of crime.

Lynn's been happier since leaving the homicide squad of LVMPD. She fit in with us at my investigating firm and was much happier being away from the grit and grime of murder and crime in Las Vegas. She also had a baby girl to take care of when she wasn't working a case. Her husband, and my friend, Deacon, had stayed with the police and had recently passed the lieutenant's test for promotion. Now he had to wait for a slot to open up.

I headed out to my Crown Vic and drove to my building to see what was going on. I parked and went in the back, setting off Lacey's cowbell on the door. I waved to the camera and went down the hallway to my office. I went in and sat at my desk and waited for Lacey, my office manager and crazy person, to come bombing in to tell me about any new cases that came in. She didn't arrive.

I waited, still no Lacey. I was getting worried and went out to the main lobby where I found Lacey sitting at her desk typing on the computer.

"Typing your resume for another job, I hope?" I asked.

"I'm answering an email for you. It's from a group in New York that wants you to come out to a book convention to speak on your success as a writer and private investigator. I'm filling in the background information on your career in crime fighting."

"And how do you know what to write?" I asked.

She lifted my latest book and said, "I'm just copying what you wrote in your bio from your book. It's nice when you have it all made out for me."

"So, why do you think I will accept this invitation to go out to New York for a book convention?"

"Because you love the attention and if you don't, I'll shoot you."

"I guess that's two good reasons. Where is this email that invited me?"

She lifted a paper from her desk and handed it over to me. It was a copy of the email that came to the firm. It wasn't even personally sent to me, although it did acknowledge me as the recipient. I read it over and was thinking about what they said would be an all-expenses paid visit to New York City. That intrigued me. If Penny could get the time off from her show, I'd accept. But Lacey already did that for me.

"This says that it will be over the four day Labor Day weekend. Maybe Penny could take the time off," I said to no one in particular. I looked at Lacey and said, "Penny and I just got back from my reunion last month in Michigan. I don't know about jumping across the country again so soon."

"As I said, you need to go there. You need to get away from this office, you're beginning to bug me," Lacey said with a wry smile.

"How am I bugging you?"

"You're always moping around. Since Lynn has been helping Las Vegas police with their cases, you've been bored. You won't take a cheating spouse case…"

"I don't like those, I've had enough of them," I interrupted her.

Reunion Murders

"…And there haven't been any meaty cases to take. Earl and Trapper jump on the hard-core ones because they pay attention to who comes in. You're always in your office meditating." She tried not to laugh, just making a snorting sound.

"Fine, I'll go to New York, but you'll miss me."

"Not with a gun I won't," she said with another snort.

I gave up and went back to my office. I sat at my desk looking around the room. It was a lot bigger now that Lynn had moved into her new office. I liked my privacy, and could take a nap when I wanted to. Or as Lacey called it, meditating.

I picked up the desk phone after checking my watch to see if Penny's show had finished taping, and called her. I waited for it to ring, when I heard a ringing from outside my door. It stopped and I heard Penny on my phone saying, "Are you in your office?"

"Yes, where are you?" I had a feeling she was outside my office on her phone.

She peeked around the door and smiled. Willy came bounding in and stood up against my leg. Penny hung up and came in the room.

"So, I hear we're going to New York," she said.

"I wish Lacey would stop filling you in on my news. I wanted to tell you myself."

"Okay, I didn't hear anything from Lacey. So, what's new?"

"We're going to New York."

*

Continued in the book…

∾∾*∾∾

Jim Richards Family of Readers

Thanks to the following people who are now part of the Jim Richards Family of Readers. They have read a book or more and enjoyed them. They all volunteered to be included in the list. If you are a fan of the books, send me your full name and you will be included in future books. Send your name to murdernovels@bobmoats.com to be added here and on the website.

* Achim Feifel * Al Norris * Alex Wheatley * Alexandra Delporte-Wilkinson * Amy Tapia * Andrea Bryan * Anne Shepherd * Arianda Sugar * Arlene Markowski * Ashley Augustus * Audra Hall * Barbara Hughes * Barbara Sammons * Barbara Schuler * Barbara Zirger * Beth Donohue Plenskofski * Betsy Childress * Beth Gibson * Bill Sandy * Bill Tornquist * Billie-jo Collie * Boni J Rychener * Carl Bishopric * Carla Lewis * Carole Henderson * Carolyn Conroy * Carolyn Riddle-Linington * Cassy Bailey * Chad Hudson * Charlotte L Duran * Cheryl L. Everett * Cindy Ackley Nunn * Cindy Valstad * Connie Bancroft * Corinne Kay O'Daniel * Dana Robbins Chuchran * Dana Wichita * Danielle Monique * Darren Heald * Dave Travers * David Wilkinson * DeAnn Jannereth * Deanna Miller * Deb Breuker Balbo * Debbie Carter * Debbie White * Deborah Fartuch * Deborah Gauze * Deborah Sullivan * Dee King * Denise Freeman * Diana Carver * Dixie Beck * Donna Gould * Donna Thompson * Donny Minter * Doris Kight * Eddie Moore

Bob Moats

* Eric Walters * Felicia Annette Bradfield * Francine
Menor * Gail Chesney * Georgiann Minster * George
Conner * Greg Colucci * Hayley Rankin * Harold Garcia
* Heidi Arnold * Irma Ranee Coy * Jacqueline Moss *
Jan Kimball * Janice Schneider * Janice Spoor * Jennifer
Redmond * Jessica Keown-Belous * Jim Beck * Jo
Boguslaw * Jo Turner * Joanne Marie Turner * John
Peiffer * John Wisbiski * Joseph Wauro * Joyce Stacy *
Joyce Trifiletti * Judy Franklin * Judy Travers * Judy
Padgett * Julie Heath * Junnahvee Benson * Karen Dahl *
Karen Grams * Karen Higham * Karen Kaiser * Karen
Meinburg Richwine * Karen Kirkman Parker * Karin
Hawkins * Karin Vasvari * Kathleen Donohue Roesing *
Kathleen Riddle-Wolfe * Kathy Hinds Moore * Kathy
Jones * Kathy Mitchell * Katie Benzler * Kay Burns *
Kelly Garcia * Ken Boggs * Keota Rodriguez * Kiera
Mccarthy * Kim Estes * Kitty Stolle * Kristie Sciler *
Kirsty Stanton * LaLonnie Scallen * Larry Morris *
Leann Parr * Lenora Scales * Leslie Marie Jackson *
Linda Forester * Linda Ingle Cox * Linda Kennerö *
Linda Magill * Lisa Bower * Liz Gibson * Lorraine
Wiman * Loretta Alexander * Lynda Bowles * Lynette
Lawrance * LuAnn Louttit * Manny Rothman * Marcia
Gibson DeWitt * Marie Calder * Marlene Bryan *
MaryLouise Kramp * Mary Lynn Gross * Megan Atkins *
Meghan Hyden * Melody Cannavan * Michael Carruthers
* Michael Dinkens * Michael Vannoy * Michelle Burns-
Mitchell * Michelle Pilcher * Micki Potter * Mike Moats
* Mimi Baur * Myrna Hecht * Nadine Sutton * Natalie
Quine * Neena Martin * O'Della Wilson * Pat Pollington
* Pat Rohn * Patricia Jarmon * Patricia C Trezza * Patrick
Barry * Paul Lawrance * Peggy Davis * Phyllis Bassett *
Raylene Matheny * Rebecca Collins Besner * Renee
Brumley * Reta Hanna * Reta Moats * Roberta Navarro-
Harder * Sally Berneathy * Sally Hubler * Sarah Santos *

Reunion Murders

Thank you to all these wonderful people.

Thank you for purchasing this book. I hope you enjoy it as much as I enjoyed writing it for my faithful readers. Please feel free to email me to tell me what you thought about my stories. I love hearing from the readers. I can be reached at murdernovels@bobmoats.com thanks again!

*